DEATH IN REHOBOTH BEACH

The Secret of the Yellow Pajamas

An
Emily Menotti
Mystery

by

MARYELLEN WINKLER

Also by Maryellen Winkler:

The Disappearance of Darcie Malone

What Killed Rosie?

Cruising to Death

Murder on the Brandywine

Death in Rehoboth Beach
Copyright 2020, Maryellen Winkler
All rights reserved.

ISBN
978-1-935751-12-0 (Paperback)
978-1-935751-22-9 (eBook)

Published by
Scribbulations LLC
Kennett Square, Pennsylvania
U.S.A.

Dedication

This book is dedicated
to my sister, Peg,
and
to the loving memory of
Paul F. Winkler
6/29/40–11/4/01

Acknowledgments

I would like to thank my friend, Donna Moe,
who once again agreed to be my First Look editor,
and Grace Spampinato, my editor,
who offered invaluable support and advice.

2001

AUGUST 25 – SEPTEMBER 1

SATURDAY

CHAPTER ONE
THE SKINNARDS

The house was waiting for them, squatting twenty yards back from Oak Avenue, two blocks west of the brooding Atlantic. The exterior was coffee-stained cedar with burgundy trim at the windows and doors. The roof peaked sharply in the front, with sides sloping off to the right and left. Dark gingerbread scrollwork outlined the eaves, creating a sad drooping mien to the home. Exuding loneliness, it slept there nestled under a stand of pines so dense that sunlight rarely broke through. Local folk referred to it as Chalet House.

Helen shivered at the sight of it. Standing in the driveway, she heard the black clouds rumble above the evergreens and watched the clouds blot out the sun.

"I hear thunder," Angie called from the car. In her voice, an undercurrent of fear trembled just beneath that last word.

"I'll get the suitcases; you get the groceries," her brother, Keith, called as he opened the trunk of his ancient Volvo. "Arthur is helping Dad into his wheelchair."

Helen turned and spoke to her younger sister, who was gathering up bags of food from the backseat of her SUV. "Between you and me, we should be able to do it all in three trips. These old shoulders of mine can still handle two bags at a time."

Helen got to the front door just as Keith finished with the two locks: one in the handle and one a dead bolt set two inches above it. Once the door gave way, he picked up a suitcase in each hand and pushed the door in with his foot.

The smell stopped them immediately: the bouquet of accumulated dust and mold of an old home that sits unoccupied for nine months of the year.

"Ugh," said Keith. "I thought the cleaners would have aired it out. Just let me put these bags down and I'll open some windows."

In the unlit gloom, it took him a moment to find the dining room table and deposit the bags.

Double windows sat on either side of the front door. Keith went to one and then the other, pushing back curtains and pulling up the stiff lower casements. His back ached with the effort, but he succeeded in raising them halfway.

The outside summer air, although hot and damp with the expectant rain, was a welcome replacement for the fetid indoor smells. A slight breeze wafted in, and weak outdoor light found purchase in the great room, illuminating the combination kitchen, dining, and living area.

Angie put two grocery bags on the table and stood next to Helen.

"Did we wander into a gothic novel?" Angie asked. "Everything is so dark and gloomy. I think this furniture is left over from the 1800s. Isn't this the same dining room table we ate at when we stayed here as children? You'd think the owners would have updated at some point."

The sisters looked with dismay at mahogany chairs with maroon cushions, a battered sofa of worn velvet, and a tall sideboard of carved black walnut.

"I expect to hear the moaning of Madeline Usher rising from her tomb any moment now," sighed Angie.

"We come here every other year," Helen teased her, "and every time you act as if we haven't been here in forty years. Be careful, or I'll think you're getting senile."

Angie paused and shivered with the thought that, at her age, it was a possibility.

Helen ran her finger along the tops of the wood chairs. "No dust," she said. "I guess it's clean."

"But what about the ghosts, Helen? Doesn't it feel like someone else is here?"

"We'll have to wait until midnight," Helen joked. "That's when they appear. Now let's get the rest of the groceries."

As they left the house, a door slammed on the second floor, and a bedroom clock that had been silent suddenly began to tick the seconds softly. Outside, the wind rushed around the eaves and rattled the attic timbers. Inside, a spirit awoke and sensed the presence of heart-beating life invading his retreat. And not just any life. He knew these visitors. This was family.

CHAPTER TWO
FOUR FRIENDS

Next door to Chalet House sat a gray-shingled saltbox with white shutters and a black roof. Like its neighbor, it was a weekly rental in the resort town of Rehoboth Beach, Delaware. Unlike its neighbor, it had a small sign tacked up by the front door with the cottage's name, Suits Us.

Late Saturday afternoon, two middle-aged couples pulled into the driveway.

Chatting and laughing, they explored their temporary home.

"A dishwasher!" Emily shouted from the kitchen. "What a bonus!"

"A side-by-side refrigerator," remarked Melinda. "I'm so happy. Lots of room for cold drinks."

"I like that everything is sparkling clean," said Bob, Emily's boyfriend.

"I like that the beds are both queen-sized," shouted Melinda's boyfriend, Elvis, from upstairs.

Bringing in the last suitcase, Bob said, "I wonder who our neighbors are in that chalet-looking house next door. Should we ask them over for drinks after we've unpacked?"

"Not just yet," Emily responded. "Let's just have a drink among the four of us and then go out for dinner."

"Yes," agreed Melinda. "You never know what kind of crazies might be next door. Let's just celebrate among ourselves."

"Done," said Elvis. He pointed the bottle of champagne away from himself as he skillfully dislodged the cork. The quick rush of carbonated air quivered with a loud "pop." Then he poured some bubbly into four fluted glasses and handed them around. "Here's to our next adventure," he said and winked at Melinda.

"Here, here," echoed the other three.

Emily added, "May this be a vacation we never forget."

The scream woke them in the middle of the night—a woman's scream, harsh and shrill as fingernails on a blackboard. Melinda and Elvis came running out into the hallway from one bedroom, Emily and Bob from another.

"Where did *that* come from?" Emily asked.

"Next door, I think," Bob answered.

They padded on bare feet into Elvis and Melinda's room, pulled back the curtains, and looked out at Chalet House next door. All seemed quiet. The scream had not been followed by a second.

"Should we call the police?" asked Emily.

Before anyone could answer, the front door of Chalet House burst open and a woman ran out, silver hair in tangles and thin arms akimbo.

"Help!" she cried. Then she stood still, looking like an ancient wraith in a loose gown and bare feet.

The four friends ran for tee shirts and pants, then hurried down the stairs and outside into the humid night.

Bob was the first to reach her. "What's wrong?" he asked, taking her tiny hands gently into his.

"Someone's going to die," she gasped.

The others quickly gathered round.

"Do you know who?" Bob asked. "Should we call the police?"

Emily put an arm around the woman's shoulders, noting the flimsy cotton of the gown covering her slender bones.

"Yes, please. Right now," the woman said. She looked up at Bob with fearful blue eyes. "There's going to be a murder!"

The woman's panic now morphed into anguish. Tears gathered in her eyes and spilled out, pausing only momentarily in the deep gullies of purple circles beneath her eyes that spoke of troubled days and sleepless nights.

"Elvis and I will go back to our cottage," Melinda said. "We'll find the phone and call the police."

"Emily, why don't you and Bob stay here to comfort her," Elvis suggested. "And talk to the police when they get here."

"That won't be necessary." A man walked toward them, a man some six inches taller than the strange woman but with the same startling blue eyes, lean build, and silver hair.

"I'm Keith, Angie's brother. We don't need the police. She's just had a bad dream. Haven't you, Ang?"

Emily withdrew her arm, and she and Bob stepped away.

"Oh, Keith. Are you sure? It was so real. Someone was dying and I couldn't help them." More tears flowed; she reached out and put both her arms around his chest.

Keith held her tenderly and offered no other explanation. The four neighbors gazed at the couple, waiting to be assured the woman was safe.

For ten seconds there was silence, then Angie whispered, "I think I want to go back to bed."

"Yes, that would be best. Don't worry. It'll be okay," her brother promised.

The four friends exchanged puzzled looks, hoping he was right. They were reluctant to move. *Was* the woman going to be alright?

"I'm sorry we disturbed your sleep," Keith said. "Maybe we can talk sometime later. We're the Skinnards, and we bring our father here every other year or so for a vacation. I'm going to take Angie inside now. Thank you for coming to her aid. Good night."

Keeping his arm around her, Keith walked Angie back to their house.

Waiting just outside the doorway were another man and woman, both around the same ages as Keith and Angie. In the glow of the entryway light, the four noticed the same distinctive blue eyes and silver hair. Their grim smiles conveyed no surprise at Angie's late-night outburst.

"We're just next door if you need us," Bob called after Keith as the four turned and walked back to Suits Us.

"Welcome to Rehoboth Beach," Emily whispered to her friends.

"Anyone for a glass of wine?" asked Elvis.

"Great idea," said Bob. "I'm wide awake now."

Melinda took a bottle of pinot grigio out of the refrigerator. "Is this alright with you guys?"

"Sure," said Bob.

"Me too," agreed Elvis.

Emily took out glasses. They sat in the living room on sofas and chairs upholstered in flowered cotton.

"Our neighbors are an interesting group," Bob commented. "Do you know them?" he asked Emily.

"That's the Skinnards. I believe we just saw the four siblings. Sans spouses."

"Odd that they'd bring their father to the beach without their husbands and wives. Of course, some of them may be divorced. What do you know about them?"

"Everyone knows the Skinnards in Rehoboth."

"Do they know you?" asked Melinda.

"No. I'm just common folk. They are royalty and rich. They've owned a chain of hair salons in the Kent and Sussex counties for over fifty years or, at least, as long as there's been such a thing as a hair salon. Perhaps I should say did own, as most of them have been sold now because the younger generation doesn't want to be in the beauty business."

"So, tell us more about our neighbors," urged Elvis, pouring himself a second glass of wine.

"You might have noticed the older man and woman observing us from the doorway. That was Arthur and Helen. I recognize them from newspaper articles about philanthropic events one or the other is always attending. Arthur is the eldest brother and still owns a salon or two in Dover. He's probably in his sixties. Helen is the oldest daughter, maybe in her fifties. The man we didn't see is their father. He's must be in his nineties."

"And the mother?" Melinda asked.

"She passed away some years ago. And there was a third brother, in between Arthur and Keith, who died in a motorcycle accident back in the eighties. What I'm wondering is where the spouses are. I know some of the siblings are married."

"How many bedrooms does that house have? Do you know, Emily?" asked Bob.

"Probably three, like this one."

"If the house only has three bedrooms, the father might have his own, Helen and Angie would share one, that leaves Arthur and Keith in the third. Not much room for spouses. I think it's rather nice that the siblings are spending some quality time as a family with their dad. He looked so old and frail when I caught a glimpse of him yesterday. He probably hasn't long to live." Bob continued thoughtfully, "My experience is that multiple spouses on vacation living under the same roof can create a lot of tension, so it's probably for the best to leave them home."

"Do tell?" Emily prodded with a smile. Bob had told her little of his previous marriage.

"My ex and I once went on vacation with three other couples.

Four women, two bathrooms, one kitchen, and bad weather that kept us off the beach. It was a disaster."

"You survived?"

"Just barely."

"Were you all related like our siblings next door?"

"Yes. Trust me. Even without Angie's outburst, we'll be lucky if no one's dead next door by the end of the week."

"You're joking, of course."

"Of course. My siblings and I all survived. Just one divorce— mine. And that was a blessing. Otherwise, I wouldn't have gotten to know you." He reached over and squeezed Emily's hand for emphasis.

"Why do you suppose Angie thinks someone is going to be murdered?" asked Elvis.

"Maybe she's planning on killing someone," Bob joked.

"No, no! Not that sweet little woman," cried Emily, looking directly at Melinda.

"I didn't have much time to study her," Melinda said, "but I didn't get any homicidal thoughts. She seemed terrified. She wanted us to help."

The others smiled. Melinda's empathic abilities were well established among the foursome.

"When do you think she imagined this murder is going to happen?" asked Elvis.

"That I can't tell you," Melinda answered.

"Any idea who the victim might be?" asked Bob.

"No," replied Melinda.

"Perhaps we should get to know them better," suggested Emily.

"What can we do?" Elvis shrugged. "They didn't seem too friendly."

"We can at least drop by and, while we're chatting, ask questions," Emily said.

"Oh no!" Bob quipped. "Looks like this won't be a relaxing vacation."

"I think I'm tired enough to sleep now," Melinda said. She poked Elvis with her elbow. "How about you?"

"Yes, ma'am. I'm with you."

The two rose and bid "Good night" to Emily and Bob.

"Us too?" asked Bob.

"Yes, but I'm not sure I'll go to sleep right away," Emily replied. "I've got to come up with some ideas of how to get to know the Skinnards better."

"And you will," Bob assured her. They gathered up the wine glasses and put them in the kitchen then went upstairs to bed.

SUNDAY

CHAPTER THREE

THE PURSE

At 7 a.m., Emily was sitting cross-legged on the living room floor. Her friends were still sleeping. She was used to rising early, finding solace in the peacefulness of the early morning. Once or twice a week, she would sit like this and meditate for a few moments on how happy she was at this point in her life, giving thanks to God or fate or whatever power governed her life. She had a best friend, Melinda, and a budding relationship with Bob. She was content in her job, and she loved her narrow townhome with its large windows that brought in sunlight and her cozy fireplace that provided warmth.

She was engrossed in these thoughts when she felt a light touch on her left shoulder. She opened her eyes and turned her head to see who had come downstairs, but there was no one. Thinking she had felt a draft, she closed her eyes.

A gentle tap, this one more insistent, touched her left shoulder once again. Emily opened her eyes and looked around for the second time. No one was there. A chill shot through her and she hugged herself for extra warmth. *The air conditioning just came on*, she thought. She closed her eyes again.

A third tap. Now, Emily felt a stab of panic. What was happening? She opened her eyes and saw him, a translucent figure, a young man in blue jeans and tee shirt, with brown, shoulder-length hair and tortoiseshell frames around his eyes.

Emily was too frightened to move. Here was a ghost, but of whom? She didn't recognize the blurry form before her.

What do you want? She silently asked him.

In her head, she heard a garbled whisper, *Hell...hell...*, then he turned his back on her and began to walk away.

Are you asking for help? Emily silently called after him, trying to pull him back with her concentration.

There was no answer. He was gone.

Emily sat quietly for ten more minutes, thinking about what she had seen, until she heard her friends stirring upstairs. *Is he asking for help or is he telling me that he is in hell? But what is the point anyway if I don't know who he is? Should I tell the others about him?*

She decided against it for now. Melinda would understand, but the men would make light of it.

Later, for breakfast, Elvis made blueberry pancakes and fresh-squeezed orange juice from the supplies he had brought. The group seemed little worse for wear after their interrupted sleep the night before.

"Any more thoughts about what happened with Angie last night?" Emily asked Melinda.

"No. Maybe she had a bad dream. A dream can be so vivid. Haven't you ever woken up from a dream thinking it was real?"

"In college, I woke up from a dream thinking I had overslept and missed an exam," Elvis said. "I ran to my classroom. Luckily, I was early and hadn't missed it."

"I think being here is reawakening some uncomfortable memories for Angie," Melinda reflected. "She's very troubled. I'll let you know if I notice anything else, with her or any of the siblings."

After eating the last pancakes and finishing off the orange juice, everyone took their coffee out to the back deck and settled into Adirondack chairs.

"What shall we do today?" Bob asked.

"Let's walk into town," proposed Emily. "I haven't been here in years. I'd like to get reacquainted with the town and visit the shops on Rehoboth Avenue. We can have lunch downtown and then decide what we want to do from there. If we're tired, we can just come home and take a nap."

"A nap!" exclaimed Elvis. "Who do you think we are, a bunch of old people?"

"Or we could just enjoy some quiet time together," Melinda winked at him.

"Oh, yes, quiet time together," Elvis repeated softly. "I'm all for that."

The others laughed.

"I think we have a plan," Bob said.

After cleaning up breakfast, Emily gathered zinnias from the garden, placing the stems in damp paper towels, and wrapped the bouquet in aluminum foil. Armed with this bouquet of red, orange, and gold blooms, Emily and Melinda went next door to see how their neighbors had recovered from the night before. They stepped out of their cool cottage into the hot breath of the August morning and walked across the macadam drive to Chalet House.

At their neighbors' door, Melinda knocked gently. Helen answered, wrapped in a blue quilted robe, her hair tousled and her smile sad but welcoming.

Emily handed her the flowers and said, "Hi! We're from next door. These are for you and your family. How are you doing this morning? I hope you all were able to get back to sleep last night."

As she spoke, she noticed Melinda staring at Helen with an odd expression on her face, as if she didn't recognize her.

"Thank you," Helen said, reaching for the flowers. "Please come in for a second. Would you like a cup of tea or coffee?"

"No, thank you," Emily replied, stepping just inside the door and noticing the others also still in their bedclothes. They were seated at the dining room table with cups and plates before them.

"We were just checking on you. Come knock on our door if you need anything."

She looked at Melinda and quickly grabbed her arm; Melinda was staring open-mouthed at the others at the table. *How can she be so rude?* Emily was thinking. She pulled Melinda by the elbow out the door, giving Helen an apologetic smile as Helen slowly shut the door behind them.

"Thank you," she heard Helen call after them.

"What is wrong with you?" she muttered to Melinda. "You were staring at her as if she had two heads!"

"Two heads? No, she didn't have two heads. But who was she? I don't remember there being any children there yesterday."

"What children? I didn't see any children."

"That was a child who answered the door. A girl. The one you gave the flowers to. She was maybe eight or nine years old."

"No, that wasn't a child. That was Helen. She's, maybe, fifty-three years old!

"That's not who I saw. And at the table—also children. Or,

rather, the boys were teenagers. And then a little girl, younger than the one you were speaking to."

"Melinda, there were no children there." Emily abruptly stopped and stared at her friend, thinking. "Wait a minute! This must be your second sight. I saw adults at the table, but you saw them as children. Have you ever done that before? Seen adults as children?"

"No. What I saw is very strange and a little upsetting. When I saw them outside last night, they were adults."

"It must have something to do with the house. When you see them outside, they're adults, but when you see them inside, they're children. What exactly did they look like? Were they happy or sad?"

"The older boy looked to be seventeen or eighteen. He had short brown hair and pale skin. He looked annoyed. The younger boy appeared to be twelve years old. He had reddish hair and a big grin. He was staring at you with interest. The little girl had blonde curly hair, and although I was too far away to see tears, I got the impression that she had been crying."

"And the one who answered the door, Helen?"

"She was blonde like the others and shy. She didn't know what to say to you. She was trying to be brave."

"Maybe, by seeing them as children, we're supposed to learn something extra about them. We'll have to go back and see if it happens again."

"My visions usually have a meaning."

"We'll find an excuse to go visit this afternoon or this evening. I can't wait to find out."

"Let's take Bob and Elvis with us just to corroborate what you and I are seeing. Please don't tell them about it just yet."

"Okay."

"I'm always afraid Elvis will change his mind about me and decide I'm crazy."

"Never."

"And you?"

"Me neither."

By late morning, the four friends were ready to take a walk downtown. The humidity had yet to descend in earnest, and they had hopes of a leisurely tour through the shops, followed by a light lunch. Then they would return home for a quiet afternoon.

Elvis appeared in plaid madras shorts whose garish colors caught them all by surprise. The interwoven threads were orange, purple, and yellow.

"Where did you find those?" Melinda teased him. "A sixties retro shop?"

"I'll have you know madras is back in style," Elvis chided her. His lean, six-foot frame did a runway walk across the living room with one hand behind his head and the other on his hip. "You obviously haven't seen the latest copy of *GQ*."

"Nor have the other folks we'll encounter on Rehoboth Avenue," Emily laughed. "But anything goes with your pure white flattop, and I do like the shorts. Be ready for a few raised eyebrows though."

"Just buy yourself a golf shirt at Carlton's," Bob advised. "Golfers can get away with wearing anything."

"So, you do know Rehoboth," Emily said.

"My parents brought me here all the time when I was a kid. I could do Funland blindfolded."

"Well, it's all new to this New England girl," Melinda said. "Let's get going."

The two couples left Suits Us holding hands. A peek to their right told them that all appeared quiet next door.

They turned left onto Oak Avenue where it was only a few steps to Second Street, with its older residential homes tucked away under towering pines. These houses were lush with well-cared-for lawns and thriving shrubbery. From Second Street, they turned right onto North First Street, where they passed less expensive homes and, later, commercial properties a little worse for the wear. Soon, they arrived at the mix of inexpensive stores and upscale shops lining Rehoboth Avenue.

"Left or right?" asked Emily.

"No politics today," admonished Elvis.

"Are you going to be the class comedian?" Melinda grinned.

"I think we need one," Elvis replied.

"Right, I think." Bob turned and pointed in that direction. "Not that I'm a conservative, but thinking geographically." He smiled. "We could do a loop. First we go up Rehoboth Avenue away from the beach, check out the shops, then cross the street and go down toward the boardwalk, then back up to here. Or we could do it the other way around."

"I second that emotion," said Emily. "I want to go to Browseabout Books and get something to read."

"Smokey Robinson?" asked Bob.

"You got it," Emily said and took his hand.

"What about lunch?" asked Melinda. "You guys know me, eternally hungry."

"Well, there's Dogfish Head Brewings or the Purple Parrot Grill," Emily said.

"Or," Bob nodded, "We could wait until we get down to the boardwalk and go to Obie's on our way back to the house. I'm going to need a nap soon afterward if I'm having an alcoholic beverage with lunch."

"Smart thinking, bro," said Elvis. "Sightsee first, eat and drink second. Let's go."

The quartet turned right and headed up Rehoboth Avenue. At the bookstore, everyone spent a good twenty minutes browsing. Emily found a mystery by Donna Leon she hadn't read. Melinda picked up a book on local history, Bob a *New York Times* book of crossword puzzles, and Elvis a collection of interviews with tech company founders of the nineties. Armed with their purchases, they reconnoitered on the sidewalk, walked to Second Street, and crossed at the light to the other side of Rehoboth Avenue, the men graciously carrying their purchases.

As they strolled down the sidewalk past clothing stores selling everything from cheap tees to hundred-dollar scarves, Emily and Melinda occasionally paused and gestured at a window display. Bob pulled Elvis aside and, heads together, spoke quietly.

A little farther along, Emily and Melinda stopped in front of a store that displayed handwoven sweaters. Bob stared at a jewelry store close by.

"Emily, I'm just going to duck in that jewelry store and see if I can pick up a birthday present for my boss. Okay?"

"Sure."

"I'll go with him," Elvis said. The two men disappeared.

"That's odd," Melinda murmured to Emily.

Before Emily could reply, Helen and Angie came out of the store in front of them. The two pairs of women seemed a bit surprised to see each other, then smiled and exchanged hellos.

"I don't think we got everyone's name last night or this morning," Emily said. "I'm Emily and this is my friend Melinda.

We've rented the cottage next door for this week with our friends Bob and Elvis."

"Pleased to meet you," Angie replied, nodding at them both. "I'm Angie, as you know, and this is my sister Helen."

"Doing some shopping, I see," Emily said, pointing to the white plastic bag Helen was holding with the store's logo in bold pink.

"Yes, it's been a successful morning," Helen replied, and then suddenly stopped and frowned. She pointed at Emily's purse, a brown leather bag with a shoulder strap and an oval flap over the opening.

"Do you mind if I ask you where you got that bag? I used to have one just like it when I was a teenager."

"I guess these bags never go out of style. I bought it years ago at a yard sale. It's hard to find real leather purses these days for under eighty or ninety dollars. Where did you get yours?"

Helen looked at her sister. Angie shook her head.

"It's not something we like to talk about," Helen said. She continued, "See that flap that covers the opening. Does it have a little zippered section on the underside?"

"I never thought to look," Emily said and pulled up the flap. There it was. A small three-inch zipper. She began to open it. The zipper was a bit rusty and resisted at first. After some effort, it slid open. She dug her thumb and index finger inside and pulled out a yellowed movie stub, crumpled and falling apart. She spread it out on her left palm and smoothed it with her right index finger. She could just barely make out "Loew's."

"That's mine!" Helen gasped. "That's my purse; that's my movie stub! I went to Loew's theater on a date with Danny Petersen when I was fifteen. How amazing is it that you would buy it at a garage sale years later? I need to sit down. This is too much."

Rehoboth Avenue was lined with hardwood benches for weary shoppers. The four women sat down while Helen and Emily both touched the purse and looked at each other.

No one spoke for a moment as chattering crowds wandered by with gayly colored bags, ice cream cones, and bulky strollers.

Smiling, Emily pleaded, "This is such an unbelievable coincidence. Now you have to tell me where you originally got this purse. From the look you exchanged with Angie, there's a story of some kind."

"It's not a good story," confessed Angie. "Not one we like to remember."

"What could possibly be bad about a new purse?"

"It's who gave it to us," Helen explained. "You see, the woman was a hairdresser in one of my father's beauty salons."

"Start from the beginning," insisted Angie, twisting her hands in her lap.

"We were teenagers," Helen began. "On a Saturday afternoon, just before Christmas, we were upstairs in our bedrooms, when our Mom came up and said someone had come to see us with a present for each of us. The oddest thing was that she made a point of telling us that we were not to ask any questions about the gifts or to act in any way like we were not grateful. We were to simply open the gifts, thank the woman, and go back upstairs."

"And that's what we did," Angie said. "We went downstairs. I remember we didn't even go all the way down to the first floor. My father and the woman were in the front hallway, and we stood on the stairs—my mother and us on the second and third steps. We knew who the woman was because she worked in one of the beauty salons. Her name was Theresa Jones."

"She handed us each a wrapped box and we opened them," Helen continued the story. "Angie and I each got a leather purse. I got the one you're using now. We thanked her for the gifts, and then we went back upstairs."

"Was it odd for one of the hairdressers to give you gifts?" Emily asked.

"Very odd. But we were dumb teenagers and didn't think anything about it," said Helen.

"Did you ask your mother about it?"

"No, but I remember she seemed rather upset by it. However, our mother was often upset with our father, so that wasn't anything out of the ordinary either."

Both women frowned.

"I never forgot that incident," Helen went on. "And when I was old enough to understand more about my father and mother, I realized that Theresa Jones was probably a woman with whom my father was having an affair. In fact, that particular hairdresser often sent candy and small gifts home to Angie and me when we were little. The purse was the only expensive gift, and I imagine my mother made sure it didn't happen again."

"What did that cost our mother?" Angie mused.

She spoke so softly Emily almost didn't hear her. She caught

Helen shaking her head and putting a finger to her lips.

"Well, here are your menfolk," Angie said suddenly, "And they've got sneaky grins on their faces. I imagine they have a surprise for you."

"I hope so," Melinda said, as Elvis and Bob joined them. "What's up, guys? What nefarious deeds have you been plotting?"

"Oh, nothing much," said Bob. "Hi, neighbors. How's everything with you?"

"We're fine," Helen answered. "On our way home to make lunch for our father. Would you like to go out for dinner with us tomorrow night? We have a reservation at Irish Airs in Lewes. I can change it to add four more. Monday night won't be too crowded since the weekend visitors will have gone home."

The couples looked at each and nodded all around.

"Great," said Helen. "Meet you there at six?"

"Wonderful," said Emily. "See you then."

CHAPTER FOUR
THE GARAGE DOOR

The four continued east on Rehoboth Avenue toward the ocean. Emily softly said to Melinda, "You saw them as adults, right?"

"Yes, not children."

"Good. It must have something to do with the house."

They passed dozens of bathing suit and souvenir stores. Coming upon a group of candy and soft ice cream shops soon had them thinking of lunch. When they reached the end of Rehoboth Avenue, they entered the boardwalk built along the dunes. Melinda was suddenly off, with her sandals in hand, skipping over the sand on her way to the ocean.

"I've never seen such a beautiful big beach!" she called out, as the others ran to catch up with her. When they did, Melinda was dancing in the shallows created by the low waves that were breaking a few yards out. The other three, being staid old adults used to the mid-Atlantic charms, only watched with amusement. But Melinda's joy was catching, and soon they, too, had removed their shoes and were dipping their feet in the cold surf.

"The water is so much warmer here!" Melinda exclaimed. "It's bath water compared to the North Atlantic."

For fifteen minutes the four stood and enjoyed the ebb and flow of the sea while nearby toddlers squealed in their parents' arms and children dug for sand crabs. A bevy of young girls in bikinis cautiously crept out to the breakers while tanned young men dove headfirst into the waves to impress them. The sun was gloriously warm on their shoulders without being too hot, compliments of a cooling offshore breeze. Mother Nature seemed at her most benevolent. Emily and Bob held hands, and Elvis made several attempts to splash Melinda, but she always managed to escape him at the last minute with a leap and a giggle. If one didn't know better, one would have thought they were fifteen, instead of mature adults.

At last Melinda slowed down and announced, "I'm hungry."

"Me too," Elvis agreed.

Tired now, the foursome headed back across the beach to the boardwalk.

"Did we decide where to eat?" asked Melinda.

"Obie's," Emily replied. "It's right on the boardwalk. They have great sandwiches, and they won't mind our sandy feet."

Back on the boards, they passed the old Atlantic Sands Hotel and the newer Victorian-styled Boardwalk Plaza before coming to Obie's By the Sea. They voted to take four seats outside under an umbrella where they could enjoy the sea breeze. It also afforded them great people watching of the sizable crowd walking up and down the boardwalk at lunchtime.

The guys ordered beer, the women, iced tea. All had a taste for burgers and fries. They dove into their food and didn't speak until the worst of their hunger had been satisfied. Emily, gazing down the boardwalk, turned to Bob.

"Do you remember the nor'easter of '62 when the Atlantic Sands lost a whole section of their hotel? My father drove down here the next day. It happened on Ash Wednesday, and he was here on Thursday morning."

"I remember my parents talking about that," he replied. "It was in the newspaper."

"Back then, the hotel was built in the shape of an L," Emily explained, addressing everyone at the table and forming the L-shape with her hands. "The long part of the L is the part you can still see. The base of the L stretched out almost to the boardwalk. The rooms had exposed doors painted different colors: red, blue, yellow. I thought it was such a pretty place." She paused, remembering.

"When my father got here that day, the base had been totally torn off by the wind like an arm ripped off from the body. Dangling plumbing fixtures and electrical wires were hanging loose in the air, unattached to the rooms that had been washed away. They never rebuilt that section. I guess they figured it was too vulnerable to storm damage."

"Understandable," said Bob, "considering how many hurricanes blow up and down the Atlantic coast."

They resumed eating, only to be interrupted by Elvis calling,

"Hello, neighbors! How are you today?"

Arthur and Keith Skinnard were just passing by on the boardwalk and were momentarily stunned to hear someone call out to them. They walked over to Obie's and smiled pleasantly when they saw who had accosted them.

"Come have a beer," Emily said.

The brothers looked at each other quickly for agreement, then Arthur said, "I think we will."

Elvis found two empty chairs, which he drew up to the table between himself and Bob.

"By the way," he said, "I'm Elvis. The redhead is my girlfriend Melinda. And these two are Bob and Emily. How's everything at the Skinnard household today?"

Keith introduced himself and Arthur, then added, "We're all good. My father's down for his afternoon nap, so we're all scattering in different directions to enjoy ourselves for a little while."

"I've lost my favorite baseball cap already," Arthur groused. "We spent two hours this morning turning the place upside down to look for it."

"I gave Arthur a Phillies baseball cap for Christmas last year," Keith explained. "I'm not going to buy him another one."

"I know I put it on the coat rack last night," Arthur said, looking bewildered. "Who would take it? Certainly not the girls."

"It'll turn up," Keith assured him.

"Yeah, probably on the last day when we're packing. What a pisser."

"Do you like the beach?" Emily asked.

"I don't care for the sand and the sunburn," Arthur said. "I had enough of that as a kid. But I like to walk on the boardwalk and get popcorn or an ice cream cone."

"Me too," Keith agreed. "I don't get to see my brother too often. I sold my shops, and now I have an accounting firm in West Chester."

"We saw your sisters earlier on Rehoboth Avenue," Emily said. "They invited us to dinner tomorrow night at Irish Airs. Is that okay?"

"They told us, and yes, that's great," said Arthur. "Sometimes we run out of conversation with Dad. Now we'll have new people to talk to."

The waiter appeared, and Arthur and Keith ordered beers.

When the waiter left, Melinda said, "It must be nice to have so many siblings. I'm an only child. I would have loved to have had so many brothers and sisters."

"Helen might disagree with you," Keith said and started to chuckle. He looked at Arthur, who was smiling also.

"What?" asked Melinda. "Were you mean to her?"

"Well, we did get her in trouble once in a while."

"How?" asked Emily.

"It's ancient history," Arthur said.

"Come on, you have to tell us now," Melinda prodded.

"Should we?" Keith looked at Arthur.

"I think you have to," Arthur replied.

"Okay, but it does make us look bad."

"Not me," Arthur said. "I wasn't there."

"You were never there," Keith said.

"I made a point of not being there. If I was, I was put to work. Now tell one of our stories. I'll get you another beer when the waiter comes back. In fact, I'll get us all another round."

"Sounds good to me," replied Elvis.

As if on cue, their waiter appeared with beers for Arthur and Keith. Elvis and Bob ordered more for themselves. The women, in the spirit of comradery, decided to join the men and also ordered beer.

"Okay," Keith began. "One summer afternoon when I was about eight and Helen was about five, I was in the backyard. I had just painted a small table red. Now, one thing you have to know about Helen is that she always wanted to be included with the boys. I mean, she had three older brothers..."

"Wait," Emily interrupted. "Tell us about the third brother. I've only met two so far."

"We had a brother, Frank, who died in a motorcycle accident in 1981. We don't talk about him much. Anyway, Helen always got angry when we were allowed to do something, like stay out after dark or go duck hunting with Dad, and she wasn't allowed because she was a girl. She tried to be tough like a boy and would do anything she was dared to do, like steal Christmas cookies from the basement that were baked special for company or peek in Mom and Dad's drawers when they weren't home. She thought she could change the way she was treated." Keith chuckled.

"We guys had told her that a real boy would never back down

from a dare, so she would do some pretty stupid things to prove she was as good as us. One of my favorites is that we dared her to tell dirty jokes she'd learned on the street at the dinner table." Now laughing, Keith said, "She didn't have a clue what the jokes were about. Mom and Dad wanted to discourage her, so they told us we weren't allowed to laugh at her dirty jokes. She would sit there so innocently saying the filthiest things, having no idea what she was talking about, and we'd be busting a gut trying not to laugh."

Arthur and Keith were both howling, remembering how they'd embarrassed their sister.

"The only joke I can remember had something to do with a man, a woman, a cave, and a flashlight." Keith was whooping so hard here he almost lost his mouthful of beer, remembering a little blonde girl at the dinner table making everyone uncomfortable.

"Poor Helen," Melinda interrupted. "I wonder how that affected her later in life."

Arthur and Keith, lost in the hilarity, didn't respond.

"Back to the garage," Arthur reminded Keith as the waiter arrived with more beer. He was accompanied by a young woman to help distribute the bottles and glasses. She wore tight white shorts, and her straight blonde hair hung down her back, nearly to the hem of her shorts.

Arthur eyed her carefully and winked at Keith as she walked away. "I'd like a piece of that action," he murmured.

Bob and Elvis politely ignored his comment.

Keith continued, "Anyway, this one afternoon, I was out in the backyard, painting a small table red. Helen had just learned how to spell her name the week before. Now, her full name is Helen Anne, and she was very proud of the fact that she could spell it completely with no mistakes. For some dumb kid reason, I told her she needed to prove to me that she could spell her name by painting it across the garage doors.

"We had a two-car garage separate from the house, and earlier that week, our father had painted the garage doors white. I thought it would be funny if she painted Helen Anne in red paint on the white doors. She didn't want to, but I dared her to do it, so then she had to do it to prove she was as good as a boy.

"Now, maybe I thought she would do it in three- or four-inch letters, and I didn't consider how big the paintbrush was. At her age, she didn't have much in the way of small muscle control.

Anyway, she takes the paintbrush and the can of red paint, and she paints 'Helen Anne' in giant letters, maybe twelve inches tall, going clear across the doors in bright red paint! When I saw what she was doing, I knew she was in for a whipping when Dad came home and, maybe, me too. I took off out of there and didn't come back for the rest of the day."

"Where did you go?" Arthur asked.

"I don't even remember. Probably Johnny's house. I would have called later and asked Mom when I could come home. Some things you block out. Maybe I got a whipping, and maybe I didn't. I got one for other things, but they kind of blur together. Do *you* remember what happened that time?" he asked Arthur.

"No, but I probably did the same as you. Took one look at those doors and hightailed it out of there."

"Did Helen get punished?" asked Emily.

"I'm sure she did—poor kid—but I wasn't there to find out. You'll have to ask her sometime. The next time I saw the garage doors, they were white again. It must have taken quite a few coats of paint to cover up that red. That's all I know. Well, we better get back," Keith said, glancing at his watch. "See you guys tomorrow night."

"Not so fast," Arthur said, putting a hand on Keith's shoulder to keep him from getting up. "Look who's walking past us on the far side of the boardwalk. Isn't that Merv the Perv?"

Everyone at the table turned to look, and there was only one person in the crowd that so perfectly fit the sobriquet. He was short, with pitch-black greasy hair combed down to his collar. The evenness of the color hinted at hair dye. His face was tan and heavily lined, suggesting an age of seventy-five to eighty. He was painfully thin and wore a cheap white dress shirt with the first four buttons undone, and wrinkled polyester pants of dingy green. He appeared to be in a hurry as he wove his way in between the mothers and fathers, children, and lovers thronging the boardwalk.

"Who's he?" asked Emily.

"Mervin Crippens, an old friend of our father's," Keith replied. "None of us liked him. He was usually drunk, and his breath could kill at fifteen feet."

"I haven't seen him in twenty years," Arthur remarked. "I thought, or maybe hoped, he was dead."

"Why do you dislike him so much, other than that he was a drunk?" Emily was puzzled.

"He was a Boy Scout leader—briefly. When stories started circulating about his activities on weekend camping trips, our father saw to it that he lost his position with the Scouts. They stayed friends though. I don't know why."

"I recall Mom saying he wasn't allowed in our house," Keith said.

"Can't blame her if what you say is true," said Bob.

"Well, he's way ahead of us now. Let's go, Keith." Arthur got up to leave, followed by his brother. They left a twenty on the table for the beer and Elvis handed it back to them.

"We enjoyed your company too much to let you pay for the beer. Looking forward to tomorrow night."

"Thanks," Keith said. "See you then."

"What a family!" Emily gasped when they were out of earshot. "A father that cheated on their mother and even brought the girlfriend home with Christmas presents, and brothers that tormented their sister even knowing they'd get punished."

"I can't wait to see them all together at dinner," Melinda said.

"Well, I'm ready for a short walk back and a nap," Bob announced. "Anybody else?"

"I'm with you," Elvis said and waved to the waiter for the check.

The sun burned hotly for the first block or so on their walk back. They hardly spoke and welcomed the sheltering pines, where the temperature dropped five degrees and sound was muffled beneath the thick needles and drooping boughs.

All was quiet at Chalet House across the way. The four let themselves into Suits Us and quickly decided they all needed naps after the exercise and several rounds of beer. Sun, surf, and beer had the expected result. All four were asleep in five minutes.

CHAPTER FIVE

MISSING

The four slowly awoke and wandered downstairs between four thirty and five. Since they had, so far, failed to visit the grocery store for dinner supplies, they unanimously decided that no one felt like cooking. They had cheese and crackers, beer, and wine but no chicken, steak, or veggies.

"Let's not go out to eat," Emily said. "The traffic on Route 1, from folks returning home from vacation and the weekend, will be horrible."

"Delivery?" suggested Elvis.

"Pizza!" sang out Melinda. "I haven't had pizza in ages."

"It's got to be Grotto's," said Bob.

"What's Grotto's?" asked Melinda. "Is that someone's name?"

"Only the place with the best pizza you ever ate," Emily told her. "I don't know how it got its name, but it started as a takeout stand, opened back in the sixties by a high school biology teacher."

"Now they're a restaurant with quite a few locations," Bob added.

"What makes their pizza so special?" Melinda asked.

"I think it has something to do with the cheese," Emily said. "It tastes different than other pizza cheeses. Whatever it is, it's my favorite."

"So we're calling Grotto's?" Bob asked.

"Maybe not. I just remembered,"—Emily pointed with her thumb—"there's a phone on the wall in the kitchen, but I haven't checked to see if it works."

"Don't bother; I'll call on my cell phone," Bob said. "Let me get it out of my suitcase."

"You have a cell phone?" Emily said. "You didn't tell me."

"They gave them to us at work last week," Bob explained and then disappeared up the stairs.

"Do you have one?" Melinda asked Elvis.

"Not yet, but I'm thinking of getting one. A lot of my clients have them now."

Bob came back with a phone that looked a bit more modern and lightweight than the others Emily had seen. It was silver and folded on top of itself.

"It's called a Clamshell, and Motorola makes it," Bob announced, flipping it up. "So find me a phone book with Grotto's number, and I'll call in our order."

Elvis found a phone book in the living room with a Grotto's ad right on the cover.

"Two pepperoni pizzas?" Bob asked as he dialed.

All agreed.

"Forty minutes," reported Bob. "They're busy tonight. Let's have a drink while we're waiting."

"I just want a soda," Emily said.

"Me too," Melinda said, nodding.

"Elvis, a beer?" Bob asked.

"Sure."

The four sat down with their drinks to watch TV. Ten minutes into the local news, there was a knock at the door. Elvis got up to answer.

It was Keith from next door. "Could I ask a favor?" he said.

"Of course. Come in. We're just sitting here watching TV."

"Would you help us walk the neighborhood and look for our father? We thought he was taking a nap, but when we went to check on him, he was gone. I'm sure he's not far. He walks slow on his own. I think we should look first before we involve the police."

"Doesn't he need a wheelchair?" asked Emily.

"Not all the time. He can walk just fine. It's the strain on his heart and lungs that his doctor is concerned about, so we try to get him to use the wheelchair as often as we can."

By the time Keith had finished talking, Melinda, Emily, and Bob were on their feet and at the door.

"We haven't met your father," Emily said. "But I'm guessing we'll know him. He's elderly, has white hair, and will be walking slowly. Do you know what he's wearing?"

"He's wearing a green knit golf shirt and plaid Bermuda shorts.

We couldn't find his loafers, so we think he's wearing those. My brother and Helen are heading down toward the ocean, and Angie is staying home in case he comes back. I'll go toward the duck pond. He always enjoys going there. And if you four could fan out downtown, that'll be a big help. We'll rendezvous back at our place in, say, forty-five minutes to an hour. If we haven't found him, then we'll call the police. Okay?"

Keith hurried off, leaving the four now slightly bewildered and casting suspicious looks at each other.

"Did they murder the old man?" Emily asked, half in jest. "And now we're being used as alibis?"

"I don't think so," Melinda said. "Keith seemed genuinely distraught."

"Then let's get going," Bob said. "How about if Emily and I search from First Street west since we're familiar with Rehoboth, and Elvis, you and Melinda search the area from First Street east to the ocean. We'll meet back here when Keith suggested. Okay?"

They all agreed and took off into the late afternoon heat, the couples holding hands and each assuring the other that they would find the old man alive and well. Would he go with strangers back to his family? They would deal with that problem when they found him.

Keith returned to the house to grab his car keys. He planned to drive slowly to the duck pond, keeping his eye out for his father. He looked on the sideboard where he was sure he had left them, but they were gone.

"Ang, have you seen my keys?"

"No, aren't they in the bowl on the sideboard?"

"No, and I haven't used them since yesterday. I'm sure I put them there."

"Well, there's no time to look for keys now. You'll have to walk to the duck pond."

"Damn it," he grumbled. "You're right. I'll leave now. Maybe they'll turn up later."

"I'll look for them while you're gone," Angie said.

Keith slammed the door as he left, sending shivers of anger into the atmosphere.

Angie shuddered and said aloud, "He probably left them in the bedroom."

The four friends retraced their steps from that morning. At Rehoboth Avenue they parted, Elvis and Melinda heading east, Bob and Emily, west.

Bob and Emily carefully walked the aisles of RB Convenience, the Seashell Shop, and Gidget's Gadgets with no sign of Mr. Skinnard. When they entered the bookstore, Emily spotted an elderly gentleman that fit his description, calmly seated in a chair and having a discussion with a man sitting next to him.

"I think that's Mr. Skinnard," Emily whispered, pointing him out to Bob. "And look who's sitting next to him." It was Mervin Crippens.

"What are we going to do now?" she asked.

"Wait until Crippens or Mr. S. leaves," Bob replied.

Suddenly Mr. Skinnard shouted, "Leave me alone, will you? How dare you follow me down here to make your empty threats. Julia's dead now. You can't hurt us."

"We'll see how empty they are," Mervin said, rising from his chair. "You'll see me again and you won't be so smug." He stood up and stalked away.

Mr. Skinnard picked up a nearby newspaper and started to read.

"I wonder what that was all about," Emily said under her breath. "How are we going to approach him now?"

"Let's just be honest with him," Bob replied. "Follow my lead."

Bob walked into the cozy area the bookstore had created for customers to relax and peruse books of interest. He sat down in a chair next to Mr. Skinnard and introduced himself.

"Mr. Skinnard, I presume," he said and held out his hand.

"Yes," said Mr. Skinnard, looking up but refusing the proffered handshake.

"I'm Bob and this is my friend Emily. We're friends of your children. We're staying right next door to you on Oak Avenue. They're worried about you. You left the house without telling them where you were going. They asked us to help find you and walk back home with you."

"I think you can see that I'm busy reading this newspaper right now."

"Let me buy you that newspaper, then you can take it home with you and read it."

"But I don't want to read it at home. I want to read it here.

Where I have peace and quiet. Those infernal children never shut up. Just like you, they're always chattering."

"I understand, sir. I won't bother you anymore. But if you don't mind, I'm just going to sit here for a few minutes and collect my thoughts."

Mr. Skinnard's eyes suddenly scrunched up in anger, and his pale cheeks erupted with scarlet blotches. His forehead turned purple with sudden rage. He hissed just loud enough for Bob and Emily to hear, "I said leave me alone, you goddamn son of a bitch!"

"Yes, sir," Bob said, backing down. He raised his eyebrows at Emily and tilted his head. He got up and moved a little way off with Emily.

Bob spoke softly to her, "You go back and tell the others where he is. I'll stay here and pretend to look at the books. I'll follow him if he gets up to leave. Okay?"

"Okay."

Emily left, feeling anxious. Would Mr. Skinnard start another scene with Bob in the bookstore? She hurriedly returned to Chalet House, where she found Melinda and Elvis talking to the siblings, and gave them the good news about finding their father. She didn't include what he'd said to Bob.

"He wants to finish reading his paper," she explained. "I'm sure they'll be back soon." This is what she said, although she wasn't at all sure that it would happen. Then a car pulled up in the driveway with a lighted Grotto's sign on its roof.

Elvis ran outside to grab the pizzas and pay the driver. Bob and Mr. Skinnard were half-forgotten as everyone grabbed a slice of pizza.

Except for Melinda, who had lost her appetite. In Chalet House, she saw the siblings as children again. Arthur and Keith were behaving like adolescents without their father around, trying to impress Elvis and the women with tales of teenage drinking binges and feats of derring-do like climbing into the girls' dorms in college for panty raids.

Arthur spoke with relish of a fraternity prank where a pledge was blindfolded, driven deep into the woods, tied to a tree, and left to free himself and find his way out.

Melinda and Emily were appalled, but Helen and Angie looked bored. They had apparently heard all this before.

Melinda noted that Helen and Angie were not taking advantage of their father's absence to be bold or talk big like their brothers. They were little girls, shrinking into the sofa cushions, as intimidated by the boys as they probably were by their father. Melinda's heart went out to them. She sensed that theirs was not a kind household for a girl child.

She was jolted from her thoughts by the anger that had crept into Arthur's voice.

"The university was no fun, you know. You got four years away from home at your party school in the Midwest. I only got two years at St. John's, and then I had to move home and commute to the university in Newark."

"Not my fault that I'm six years younger than you and four years younger than Frank. Not my fault that Dad was having money problems and couldn't afford two boys in private college at the same time."

"I'm not saying it's your fault; I'm just saying it wasn't fair. You know you were always the favorite son."

"Again, not my fault."

Emily spoke up, "I think we should go next door and wait."

Melinda and Elvis murmured agreement, and the three rose to leave.

"Please, don't go," Helen said. "They argue like this all the time." She would have continued but, then, the door opened and their father walked in. Bob hung back behind him and, seeing that Mr. Skinnard was safely home, waved to the others, turned, and returned to Suits Us to wait for the other three.

"What's for dinner?" Mr. Skinnard asked.

"Dad, where have you been?" Helen exclaimed. "You left without telling us."

"Since when does a father owe an explanation to his children?" he said. "Now, what's for dinner?"

He went to the head of the dining room table, pulled out a chair, and began to sit. As he lowered himself onto the seat of the chair, the chair was pushed out from under him and he crashed to the floor.

"Ouff!" he cried out as he hit the floor and fell backward.

Everyone rushed to him, Arthur getting there first and grabbing him by one arm, Keith by the other. Together they pulled him up and held onto him as Elvis retrieved the errant chair and positioned it under Mr. Skinnard. Arthur and Keith safely lowered their father onto the chair, and he sat down.

"What just happened?" Helen cried out. "No one was anywhere near that chair. How did it move on its own?"

Mr. Skinnard looked bewildered. "I didn't move it," he said.

The children looked at one another mystified.

"This damned house," Angie said. "It doesn't like us."

"Houses don't like or dislike people," Arthur argued. "The floor must be slippery there."

No one offered any other explanation.

Angie asked, "Are you sure you're alright, Dad? At your age, you could break a hip or crack your pelvis."

"I'm fine," he growled. "Just hungry."

"I'll fix Dad something to eat," Helen stated and went into the kitchen.

"We'll be going," Elvis said. He, Emily, and Melinda walked to the door.

"Thank you," Keith replied, saying nothing further.

Moving out of earshot from the house, Emily turned to Melinda. "What did you see? Did someone move that chair?"

"No, I didn't see anything."

When they arrived back at Suits Us, Bob was in the kitchen fixing himself a bowl of cereal.

Emily embraced and kissed him. "I'm so glad you're okay. I was worried Mr. S. might decide to do something weird like walk up and down the boardwalk all night."

"Me too. I'm guessing you guys ate all the pizza."

"'Fraid so, bro," Elvis said. "Had to keep the siblings over there distracted while we waited for the old man, speaking of which, you'll never guess what happened." And he described how the chair had been pushed out from under Mr. Skinnard.

"By the way,"—Emily took Melinda aside—"did you see the kids as adults or children?"

"Children—very unhappy children."

MONDAY

CHAPTER SIX

SISTERS

Everyone slept in Monday morning. Around ten o'clock Emily wandered downstairs, enticed by the aroma of coffee. Elvis was poised at the kitchen stove with eggs and bacon at the ready.

"We're starving," he said. "When are you sleepyheads going to come down and let me cook up some breakfast?"

"Bob will be down in a minute. I think he wanted to take a quick shower. He's quite fastidious for a guy."

"What? Are you calling me a slob?" Elvis joked, pointing to his sleeveless tee shirt and cutoff sweatpants.

"Yes, she is," Melinda shouted from the living room. "And I'm no better. I believe this is one of your old work shirts I'm wearing. We're quite the couple."

"Well, I'm still in my pajamas, so not to worry," Emily responded. "Look, here's His Highness. Start cooking, Elvis. I'm sure we're all hungry after last night, and we certainly need to go to the grocery store this morning."

"Top of the morning to you," Bob greeted them as he came downstairs in a crisp striped shirt and creased blue jeans.

"Did you iron those?" Melinda whispered to Emily as she got up off the couch to make toast.

"Never. I've forgotten how to use one. He actually enjoys ironing." She blew Bob a kiss as he passed her and settled himself down at the table.

Within minutes, Elvis had whipped up an omelet, Melinda produced toast, Emily poured juice, and the four were enjoying breakfast.

"So, grocery store today?" Bob asked.

"And liquor store?" Elvis joined in.

"How shall we divvy it up?" Emily asked. "I don't cook much, and I don't drink much either."

"Way to get out of it," Melinda joked.

"No, I'll help. Why don't you and I go to the grocery store, and we'll send the men to the liquor store?"

"Very sexist," commented Bob. "I work in Human Resources. I can recognize that right off."

"Can you now," Emily teased. "We're so lucky to have you on board. You decide, then. Who goes where? Or shall we just form a committee and all four of us will go to both places? We'll put each purchase up for a vote, and it will take all day, maybe all week, to get anything done, just like at the bank."

"Children, children," Elvis broke in. "I like Emily's original idea, sexist or not. Bob and I do most of the drinking, so I would prefer if we chose the booze. Melinda knows what ingredients I like to cook with. Bob, do you cook?"

"I grill."

"Well, I did see a grill out back, and I imagine we'll eat out a lot, so I volunteer the guys to do the cooking, and Melinda will know what to buy. Are we settled?"

Emily raised her glass of juice. "I move that we accept Elvis's proposal."

"I second it," said Bob, raising his glass. "And I'll be glad to drive. I'm loving my new MDX. Can you be ready in half an hour, Elvis?"

"If someone will do the dishes, I'll be ready in fifteen."

"I've got them, darling," said Melinda. She winked at Emily. They would take their time getting ready to go to the grocery store. What was it with these men who had to rush around even on vacation?

Sitting behind the wheel in Elvis's five-year-old RAV4, Melinda asked, "Where's the grocery store?"

"On Route 1," Emily replied. "An IGA store."

It took them only minutes to leave the tree-shaded lanes of Columbia Avenue to Route 1A and then to Route 1 itself. As they passed the Tanger Outlets on either side of the highway, Emily said, "I hope we'll have some time to go clothes shopping this week."

"I'm sure we will," Melinda answered. "You know, these are all the same shops we have at the outlets in New England. I feel right at home. Odd how, with the same shops and the same fast food outlets, it's hard to tell you're even in a different state."

"You'll know tonight when we're at dinner. Order some steamed Maryland crabs. There's nothing like them in New Hampshire. But, Melinda, I need to tell you about something that happened yesterday morning. I was downstairs meditating before you all got up and saw a ghost. The ghost of a man in blue jeans and tee shirt. I don't know who he was."

"Did he say anything?" Melinda asked.

"He whispered, but I couldn't understand him. It sounded like 'hell.' I was wondering if he was asking for help or if he was telling me that he was in hell. What do you think?"

"I've no idea. How long did the apparition last?"

"Only a few seconds. Then he faded away."

"Maybe he'll appear to you again and give you some more information."

"Can't say I'm in a hurry to be frightened again, but I guess you're right."

Arriving at the IGA, they parked, grabbed a cart, and hurried inside.

"Sure is busy," Melinda remarked as she noticed lines four and five deep at the checkout counters. "I would have thought, with the weekend folks gone, it would be less crowded."

"But the week-to-week renters have arrived and need to stock up," explained Emily. "Now what's on our list?"

"Just start up aisle one, and I'll call out what we need as we come to it."

Slowly, they made their way through the store, filling their cart with bread, English muffins, butter, coffee, lunch meat, fruit, tonic water, soda, chips, and juice.

"Wait," said Emily at one point. "We don't have anything for dinner."

"Will we be cooking dinner?" Melinda asked. "So far, we've ordered pizza, and tonight we'll be going out. Maybe we should wait and just buy what we need as we need it."

"Well, I think we should have something on hand..."

"Emily Menotti! Is that you?"

A tall woman with a salt-and-pepper bob touched Emily's elbow, and Emily turned around to see someone who looked vaguely familiar. At first, Emily couldn't place her. The puzzled look on her face prompted the woman to identify herself.

"I'm Mary Jo Feeley. I dated your brother for two years when we were in high school. Remember me now? I was over your house all the time. We used to babysit you on Saturday nights. Remember the night you tricked me into letting you use Tide for bubble bath? It took us all night to get the bubbles out of the bathtub, you naughty girl!"

Laughing, Emily said, "I do remember you! I'm so sorry! This is my friend Melinda. How are you, Mary Jo? Do you live in Rehoboth or are you just here on vacation?"

"I'm retired, or rather Dan and I are retired. I'm married to Dan Smith, so I'm Mary Jo Smith now. I met Dan a few years ago. He's from Dover, where I lived before moving to Wilmington. He was a detective with the State Police. We live in Rehoboth now over in the Pines."

"That's not far from where we're staying on Oak Avenue! We're at the cottage with the name Suits Us tacked on the front. We should get together. But if you lived in Dover, I wonder if you know our neighbors here, the Skinnards."

"Everyone knows the Skinnards. The old man built up quite a business of beauty salons and then sold most of them when he retired. I think the oldest son still owns a few. A very respectable family, but sad. The middle son, Frank, was killed in a motorcycle accident in '81. Some talk of a fight with his father right before. His motorcycle skidded off Pilottown Road during a storm. Look, I gotta run."

She scribbled her phone number on the back of her grocery list. "Here's my number; give me a call. Come over for cocktails, okay?" Mary Jo thrust the piece of paper into Emily's hand and hurried off to the checkout counters.

Emily and Melinda were left breathless by both her manner and her information.

"Thank you, Mary Jo," Emily said quietly.

"She's a gold mine," Melinda said. "We have to visit."

Emily said, "Maybe she can help us figure out who's going to die."

When Emily and Melinda returned with the groceries, they found Bob and Elvis sitting out back having a beer.

"Time for lunch, boys," Emily said. "But only after you help us bring the bags in from the car."

The four made quick work of unloading and making lunch and were soon lounging on the back patio with sandwiches and iced tea.

"I thought we might like to spend some time on the beach this afternoon," Emily suggested. "You never know what kind of weather might happen later in the week. The last weeks in August are particularly prone to hurricanes. What do you think?"

"I like the idea," Bob agreed.

"Me three," Melinda said.

"What she said," Elvis commented.

"That should be, 'Me four,'" Bob corrected, always the stickler for rules.

"Whatever," Elvis replied, "As long as my lady love will be there."

"We have to look for an umbrella. The rental agent said there would be one," Emily said.

"I'll look for an umbrella," Bob offered. "Elvis, you look for chairs."

"And I'll look for the sign we put in the car that allows us to park at the end of the street," Emily said. "I feel like I've done more walking these past two days than I usually do in a month. It'll be wonderful to sit still for a few hours and listen to the ocean." She smiled.

"I hope I brought enough sunblock," Melinda frowned. "My skin burns within minutes."

"I have plenty," Emily reassured her.

A half hour later, the four were changed into bathing suits and packed into Elvis's RAV4 along with one umbrella, four chairs, four beach towels, and a small cooler.

"Love these SUVs," Elvis said as he took the wheel. "Can you imagine carrying all this stuff three blocks down to the beach?"

"Our parents did it," Emily recalled. "But they made us carry our sand toys."

"Mine had one of those Radio Flyer wagons," Bob said. "We piled all the beach stuff in the wagon, and my father pulled it while the kids walked."

"We never went to the beach," Melinda said. "We had a pool in the backyard. But I always wanted to go."

"Poor little rich girl," Elvis teased.

Because it was early in the week, many parking spots were

available at the foot of Oak Avenue; Elvis could easily park on the street side of a beach dune. They quickly grabbed their gear, each holding a chair and a towel, with the guys also managing the cooler and umbrella between them. The four made their way over a small wooden boardwalk that passed over the dune and onto the beach.

As they crested the dune and caught sight of the cobalt blue sky rising above the emerald sea and sparkling white sand, they collectively came to a standstill.

"So beautiful," Melinda murmured.

"I've missed this," Bob said.

"Let's find a spot and put this stuff down," Elvis advised, and off they trudged again to a spot about twenty yards back from the water's edge. There they sat for three hours, soaking up all the restorative magic that sand, sun, and salt air can offer.

At Chalet House, Helen and Angie were seated on the back patio, each with a book in her hand. But their thoughts were far away from the printed pages in front of them.

Helen sipped on lemonade, while Angie nursed a martini.

"Do you know what day this is?" Angie asked.

"Yes, it's the tenth anniversary of Mom's heart attack." Helen refrained from adding "and death." She hated to be so achingly specific. Bad enough her mother was dead; she didn't want to emphasize it.

"Some days, I barely remember what she looked like," Angie sighed. "I have to go find a photograph to remind myself."

"Not me," said Helen. "I see her every morning when I look in the mirror. The only difference is that she had dark hair and mine is blonde or was blonde before the gray."

"I know I look like Dad's side of the family. The curly hair and freckles were always a curse. Do you miss her?"

"Yes. I often think of that line, 'only the good die young.' I would have preferred that we were taking care of Mom now rather than Dad. She was so sweet-tempered."

"I know. I would have moved her in with me in a heartbeat." As tears began to gather in the corners of her eyes, Angie put down her book and searched her pockets for a tissue. "And I miss hearing her play the piano or seeing her with her sewing box hemming a skirt while we watched TV. She was so calm. I wish I were more like her."

"But you are like her. You're shorter than me like she was, and you're always so aware of the right thing to do or say. I'm tall and clumsy and inarticulate." Helen paused, then continued, "Look at how devoted you are to your husband. You let his family dominate all the holidays. Just like Mom. We never saw her family except, maybe, once every couple of years. You rarely find time for us, your own family, and spend all your time cooking for Ted's."

Helen tried to keep the resentment out of her voice. Her sister and her husband were always too busy to come to her Christmas Eve family gatherings, and she felt Angie should be there. Couldn't Ted agree to one holiday with his wife's family? But, no, there was always some great tradition in Ted's family that had to be observed for each occasion. Then it dawned on Helen that perhaps Angie didn't want to celebrate Christmas with her own family. Ted's family was loving and fun, while any celebration with the Skinnards was riddled with anxiety.

"I'm sorry," Angie said, aware of her sister's feelings. "We'll try to make it to your house this Christmas."

"When I was married, at least I had my husband's family to celebrate with," Helen whined. "But now that I'm divorced, I wind up being the fifth wheel at someone else's celebration. Sorry, I don't mean to make you responsible for my problems. I know there's nothing you can do about Ted's family."

But what Helen said and what she felt were quite different. If she were honest, she knew it wasn't just Angie's in-laws that were the source of her unhappiness. Helen felt sorry for herself for not being a good enough wife to hold onto her husband and her old life.

Even though she was always the one responsible for hosting her in-laws for holiday dinners—doing all the housecleaning, buying, and cooking—she hadn't minded because she was able to create a warm, satisfying holiday get-together. She'd truly loved her husband's family, especially his sister, and was still hurt that they'd cut off all ties with her. "Loyalty," her sister-in-law explained when Helen had asked her why they couldn't stay friends. The answer did little to assuage Helen's feelings of abandonment.

"Let's try to get together more often for lunch when we get home," Angie offered. "I can delegate some of my responsibilities at the bookshop."

Suddenly Helen was struck by her neediness and was ashamed.

"That's a great idea," she said. "I'd like that."

The sisters reopened their books and began to read, though neither noticed what they were reading. They sat mired in guilt and regret, knowing each had hurt the other. As childhood allies against restrictive parental rules and abusive brothers, they had needed the emotional comfort of the other. There was no such necessity now.

"Mom always loved you best. You know that, don't you?" Angie said suddenly.

"No! Why would you say that? I never noticed any preference. But, you, the baby, were always the center of attention. You had things handed to you that I had to fight for. You always seemed to do anything you wanted to do, whether it was being out late with friends or getting a car when you went to college."

"I don't think that was love; I think that was more like keeping me quiet and out of their hair. You remember what Mom said about the day she brought me home from the hospital?"

"No, what was that?"

"She said she walked in the front door to find the girl hired to help standing there with all you four kids jumping up and down around her. She told Mom she quit. She quit right then as Mom stood there in the hall with me in her arms. The girl just walked out the door. Mom said she started to cry and didn't stop crying for two years. Does that sound like she loved me? She was stuck with me, child number five, and she hated it."

"I'd forgotten that story." Helen rose from her chair and went to hug Angie.

"I'm sorry. I can't help what Mom did or didn't do, but we all know she loved you." Helen said, returning to her chair. "And I know, too, that I was mean to you when I was little."

"Mean? You were horrible! You hit me over the head with that doll we called Hardhead, the one with the wooden head and soft body. You probably gave me a concussion."

"I know. I do sort of remember that."

"And then there was the time you cut off all my hair."

Helen smiled to herself, remembering the three-year-old Angie sitting on a rug with her blond curls in a heap on the floor.

"Well, it wasn't the end of the world," Helen said in her defense. "It all grew back. I was just trying to be nice and give you a haircut."

"No, you weren't. You were being mean. You hated me." Angie stopped to reflect on their troubled childhood.

Helen was speechless with regret. *Angie is right,* she thought. Helen had been the fourth child, a girl after three boys. She had been the baby and the princess for three special years. Then, when the new girl baby came home, Helen's reign was over.

"I am truly sorry, Ang, that you don't feel loved, but I think you're wrong to blame Mom. Blame Dad for being a sex addict or the Catholic Church for not allowing birth control. But you're wrong to blame Mom."

Helen was quiet and then added, "What can I do, Ang? I can't change the past."

Angie closed her book and got up out of her chair. "There's nothing you can do. My husband takes care of me now."

There it is, Helen thought. *We marry spouses who will make up for all the losses of our childhood.*

"I'm sorry for being cranky," Angie said, now standing above her, her mood changed. "I love you." She kissed her sister on the forehead and returned to her seat.

"Love you too," Helen replied and decided to return to the house for more lemonade. She didn't get far before she stopped in surprise at the sight of a man walking around the side of the house to the backyard.

"You are?" she asked, but it took her only another second to recognize him.

"Mervin Crippens," he said. "An old friend of your father's. Remember me?"

"Of course," Helen said, and what she remembered was that she'd never liked him. She didn't bother to offer him hospitality; she wanted him gone.

"I came by to see your father," Mervin said. "Is he here?"

"He's sleeping right now," Angie called out in reply.

"You must be Helen, and that would be little Angie over there in the chair, right?" he asked.

"Yes, but as Angie said, our father's sleeping. Can I give him a message?"

"He'll know what it's about," Mervin said. "I'll come back."

He turned around and went back the way he'd come in, under the pines and out to the front. He looked carefully at the house. A stranger would have said he was sizing it up. Then he walked out to the road and down Oak Avenue.

When Helen returned to the house, she found her father just coming down the stairs. He was moving slower than usual, with one hand on the railing and one hand on the wall to steady himself. When he reached the bottom, he stopped to catch his breath. Helen could see that he was struggling to recover from his walk down the stairs.

"Are you alright, Dad?" she asked.

"I'm fine, just not quite awake yet," he answered. He slowly put one foot in front of the other as he made his way to a stuffed chair and lowered himself gingerly into it.

"Can I get you something?" Helen asked. Her father looked paler than usual. "A glass of water? A soda?"

"Just a glass of water with some ice," Mr. Skinnard responded.

Helen was handing him the glass as Angie came in from the backyard.

"Hi, Dad," Angie said. "You just missed someone who stopped to see you. I told him you were sleeping."

"Who was it?"

"Mervin Crippens."

Mr. Skinnard's face went from pale to white. He leaned forward and set down his glass of water on the tray table next to him. With some effort he spoke in a garbled tone. "No, I don't want to see him. Don't you girls let him in this house." Then he put his hand to his heart and flopped back in the chair.

"Are you sure you're alright, Dad?" Helen asked. "Do you need to see the doctor? If you're having more problems with your heart, we can go to the emergency room."

"I'll be fine," he responded in a breathy voice. "Just let me be. And don't let that man in the house!"

"No, of course not," Helen reassured him. She gave Angie a worried look. *What now?* it said.

Angie shook her head. She had no idea what Mervin Crippens's presence foreshadowed. She didn't want to know.

CHAPTER SEVEN

CRABS

Later in the afternoon at Suits Us, there was some debate over the proper attire for dinner. Elvis pointed out that it was an Irish pub and only jeans were acceptable. His were black, topped with a black sports shirt.

"You look more like a member of the Italian Mafia," Melinda said. She sported a silky red V-neck top over white capris.

Emily and Bob admired the six-foot-tall couple. The combination of black, red, and white attire, with Elvis's pale hair and Melinda's currently magenta coif, was stunning.

Bob whistled. "Wow! What an effect!"

Bob's jeans were pale blue, and he wore a Hawaiian shirt à la Jimmy Buffet. Emily was the quiet one in a southwest patterned jersey and Levi's.

They arrived at Irish Airs promptly at 6 p.m. to find their neighbors just seconds ahead of them and being seated at a large table on the screened patio. Formal introductions were made to Mr. Richard Skinnard, in case he didn't remember them from the evening before. Mr. Skinnard looked up and recognized Bob from the bookstore. He glared at him but kept silent.

Emily leaned toward Melinda. "Adults or children?"

"Definitely adults," she replied in a whisper.

Mr. Skinnard sat in his wheelchair at one end of the table where he could look out at the canal and enjoy the view of early evening fishing boats and family sailboats making their way into the harbor. He wore a Hawaiian shirt in shades of cream and white, a sober contrast to the blue skies and orange parrots of Bob's. Arthur and Keith wore golf shirts, Arthur's green and Keith's grey. Helen had chosen a loose tan sweater with short sleeves, and Angie wore a pale green sweater with long sleeves and a loose white scarf that hid her thin neck and shoulders.

"We're wearing our new purchases," Helen told them. "How about you?" she nodded at Emily and Melinda. "Did you buy anything downtown?"

"No, I'm waiting for a trip to the outlets...," Emily started to answer but was interrupted by the waiter handing out the menus.

They were a noisy bunch. The Skinnard family had eaten at Irish Airs before, but the others hadn't, so a heated discussion ensued over what was best on the menu. Arthur argued for traditional Irish fare like Guinness Stew or Bangers and Mash. Keith liked seafood. They were, after all, at the beach, he stressed. Helen liked the wings, and Angie mentioned sandwiches like a tuna melt or a simple chicken salad. One had to admit there was plenty to choose from.

Suddenly the sound of glass ringing broke through the discussion. Mr. Skinnard was tapping his knife against his water glass. "I need a drink," he announced.

The waiter appeared instantly, no doubt alerted by Mr. Skinnard's knife-to-glass demand.

"Certainly, sir. What'll it be."

"Manhattan. Straight up."

"Yes, sir." The waiter glanced at Arthur, seated to Mr. Skinnard's right.

"Bud Light."

Helen was next. "Chardonnay."

Emily surprised them with "Guinness."

To Bob's raised eyebrows she replied, "This is an Irish pub."

"I'll have the same," he said.

Across the table Elvis piped up, "Pepsi, I'm the designated driver."

Melinda said, "I'll try the Guinness."

Angie ordered the Chardonnay, and Keith a Pepsi. "I'm also the DD tonight," he explained.

Their waiter nodded and left.

Arthur turned to his father. "So, what's it going to be tonight, Dad? Crab cakes, Irish stew, or something different?"

"I think I'll go with the stew," Mr. Skinnard said. "I haven't had a good Irish stew in a long time. What's everyone else having?"

"I'm having the stew also," Arthur replied. "My wife can't get the gravy right when she tries to make it. You spoiled us all, Dad.

You were such a good cook. Our wives just never got the hang of it." He nodded at Keith to include him.

"Speak for yourself, Art. My wife is a great cook."

"We're not talking about your wife tonight, Keith. Don't get me started on your wife. And it's a good thing our wives aren't here. This is the most relaxing vacation I've had in years."

"I love your wives," Angie interjected. "They're both so warm and friendly. No one's allowed to say anything bad about anyone's spouse tonight. I'm having the chicken salad sandwich. What are you having, Helen?"

"I'm having the wings with the mild sauce. What are you having, Keith?"

"The crab cakes. I love their crab cakes. Hey, neighbors, what have you decided on?"

Bob shocked them all by saying, "Bangers and Mash. Do you guys know what that is?"

Melinda smiled. "I've been to England. That's sausage and potatoes, right?"

"Right. I've always wanted to try it. Such a crazy name. What are you having, Melinda?"

"I'm not adventurous at all. A chicken salad sandwich sounds good to me. What about you, Elvis?"

"Irish Stew. How often do I get to order that?"

"Well, I'm having the wings, like Helen," said Emily. "I think they'll go great with my Guinness. And here it is."

The waiter appeared and proceeded to set down the beer, wine, Pepsi, and one darkly handsome manhattan in front of Mr. Skinnard. He stood still as Mr. Skinnard carefully lifted the cocktail to his lips. He sipped. He set the glass down. He frowned and looked up at the waiter.

"That's awful," he said. "I can't drink that. Take it away."

The waiter's face registered shock first, then confusion. He'd obviously never had such a reaction to a drink he'd served.

"Of course, sir. Can I get you something else?"

"Not now," Mr. Skinnard growled. "I'll drink the water."

The waiter picked up the manhattan and left.

Everyone at the table was stunned into silence and nervously sipped their drinks. They looked down at their silverware. Finally, Arthur said, "The drink was that bad, Dad?"

"Nobody knows how to make a decent manhattan these days.

They're all too lazy. They use cheap ingredients. They don't take the time to do it right. I'll probably just order a beer. They can't screw that up."

A man appeared to Mr. Skinnard's right in dark pants and a short black jacket. He was young, maybe twenty-five. He had lush dark hair combed back from his ruddy face. He angled himself so that Mr. Skinnard could see him easily.

"Sir, I'm the bartender for Irish Airs, and I understand that you were unhappy with the manhattan that I mixed for you."

Glances went across the table among the Skinnard siblings. *Here comes trouble*, they seemed to say.

"That's correct," Mr. Skinnard said.

"I want to apologize, sir."

The glances flew again. Eyebrows went up.

"You are clearly a man of some experience. I wonder if you could tell me exactly how a manhattan should be made."

This was news. Had a bartender ever apologized for a bad drink? Much less asked for mixing directions?

Mr. Skinnard was all smiles.

"I'd be glad to," he replied and launched into what many at the table found to be a fascinating explanation about the need for using rye whiskey rather than any other type and the necessity of using sweet Italian vermouth with just a dash of Angostura bitters. To his credit, the bartender seemed genuinely eager to learn that the ratio of rye to vermouth must be two to one and that the mixture must always be stirred with ice chips, not shaken, and then poured through a strainer into a chilled cocktail glass before being garnished with a maraschino cherry.

"Can I make you another one following your directions?" the bartender asked.

"Of course," said Mr. Skinnard.

The bartender left.

"How amazing was that!" Helen said. "He seemed totally sincere about learning to make the perfect manhattan."

"We'll see," said Arthur.

"Most of their customers probably order beer or wine, with an occasional request for a margarita," Keith said. "No one drinks manhattans these days."

Conversation began again about the numerous menu offerings. After five minutes, the bartender returned with a new manhattan in the appropriate glass and placed it gingerly in front of Mr. Skinnard. He stood and waited.

Mr. Skinnard lifted the glass to his lips, sipped, and smiled.

The entire table smiled with him.

"Excellent," he announced.

"On the house," said the bartender. Then he turned around and walked away.

Before anyone could comment on this extraordinary turn of events, their waiter appeared again to recite the evening's specials.

"A garden variety of crudités served on a cloud of fresh kale and radicchio."

No one smiled.

"Garlic butter baked salmon served with quinoa and fresh asparagus."

No takers.

"Jumbo steamed crabs with Old Bay Seasoning at market price."

"Which is?" Arthur asked.

"A dozen for forty-nine ninety-nine."

"Who wants to share a dozen as an appetizer?" Arthur asked.

There was a momentary silence.

"Come on, we're on vacation. At the beach. At the height of blue crab season."

"I'm good for a few," Elvis shrugged.

"I'll eat some," Keith said.

"I'll have one," Emily said. She looked at Bob.

"Too messy for me," he said.

"Get me a beer, and I'll eat a few," said Mr. Skinnard.

"I'd like to try them," said Melinda. "Will you show me how to eat them?" she asked Elvis.

"*I'll* show you all how to eat them," growled Mr. Skinnard.

"Then I'll eat one too," said Helen. "How about you, Angie?"

"No, I don't like crab. I'll just watch."

"Let me get that order in now," the waiter said. "The crabs go fast. Then I'll be back to take your orders for your entrees."

He disappeared and the diners all smiled at each other. This meal was turning out to be an adventure.

In a flash, their waiter returned with more napkins, heavy paper plates, small mallets, tiny forks, and plastic bibs. Then he took their entrée orders and disappeared again, only to returned with bowls of drawn butter.

"Now which of our beers would you like to try?" the waiter asked.

"Just a Bud will do," he replied.

"I'll be right back."

"You've eaten steamed crabs before," Melinda said to Elvis.

"All the time. During the season, my parents would bring them home on a Saturday night. My mom would spread newspaper on the porch table, and we'd sit for hours picking crabs. Occasionally, friends or relatives were invited over. I have really happy memories of those times."

"I like crab also," Helen chimed in, "But I have to admit I prefer them already prepared as crab cakes or Crab Imperial."

"Remember the time I was steaming a dozen in the kitchen and you wanted to help?" Mr. Skinnard asked her.

Helen's cheeks turned red and she looked down at her lap.

"Tell them what you did," he insisted.

"When Dad asked me to put in the Old Bay Seasoning, I got it mixed up with the box of baking soda. I mean, I was only six years old; I couldn't read. They were both yellow containers. So I dumped half a box of baking soda in the pot."

Everyone at the table fell into an uneasy silence.

Emily looked at Melinda, who was frowning.

Mr. Skinnard seemed to be a volatile person. Was he recalling a funny incident, or was he trying to shame Helen, or both? Everyone could see the siblings weren't sure either.

No one was laughing, especially not Helen.

"You needed glasses, honey," Mr. Skinnard finally said and burst out laughing. "I just had to wash off the crabs and boil up a new pot of water. It wasn't the end of the world. Don't look so solemn."

"You're right, Dad. And I did get glasses shortly after that."

The Skinnard siblings relaxed, and the somber mood was broken.

The waiter reappeared with a tray of crabs, orange shells glistening with steam. The aroma of Old Bay Seasoning teased their nostrils, and their taste buds awakened to the culinary delight about to sweeten them.

"Enjoy," their waiter said as he placed the tray in the center of the table and then motioned to another waiter who supplied Mr. Skinnard with a glass of beer. The two quickly turned around and left.

"There's a skill to picking a crab," Mr. Skinnard said as his wizened hand reached for the topmost crab from the pile. "Watch and learn."

The other six partakers each took a crab and pretended to be students of the grand master.

"First, you remove the claws and legs."

They watched him twist the two first claws gently.

"Sometimes a little meat may come out with the legs." He instructed, "You can eat it."

They did, sucking on the joint to get the most white meat out as possible.

"Put aside the claws. The skinny little legs you can throw away."

"Now turn the crab on its back and pull back the apron, that's the thing that looks like a big tab." He demonstrated. "Like this."

The table watched as he pulled on the narrow piece of shell of the crab's underbelly. It came up easily.

Mr. Skinnard continued, "Now take the top half and slowly remove it from the bottom half like you are opening it up and exposing its insides, which is what you're doing. Throw away the top half."

"Yuck!" Angie said under her breath and grimaced.

"Be quiet," Keith responded in a hushed tone. "You'll upset the old man."

Mr. Skinnard didn't appear to hear. "Next, use your fingers or a knife to remove the gills on either side of the crab. They're the feathery things. You need to get them all out."

The "feathery things" were abundant on either side of the crab's interior and did indeed resemble grey bird feathers.

Emily's reaction on seeing them was always *ugh!*

The crab eaters were doing an excellent job, although Elvis and Keith seemed to be a bit ahead of the others and were already chewing on crabmeat. No one seemed to mind. They were too intent on successfully mastering their crustacean.

"Now," continued Mr. Skinnard, "Pick up the crab and break it in half, right down the middle. As you can see, there's still lots of gooey stuff left. Just take your knife and scrape out anything that doesn't look appetizing."

"There's a lot of that," Helen commented, eyeing the unappetizing yellow liquid.

"I sometimes use a paper napkin to sop that up," Elvis offered.

"I'm a bit of a purist about the crabmeat."

"Great idea!" Keith said. "I'll try that."

"Now take your fork and pull out the crabmeat from the chambers," Mr. Skinnard advised. "That's the tastiest crab of all."

"This is delicious!" Melinda said. "Are we all done?"

"No, we still have the claws," Elvis told her, "That's what the mallets are for."

"Yes, son," Mr. Skinnard said. "You didn't let me finish."

"I'm so sorry, Mr. Skinnard. It was your show. I apologize." Emily looked up at the siblings and saw looks of concern on their faces. Had Elvis created a problem? They were literally holding their breath as if expecting an explosion.

"No, no, son. It's okay. I'm glad to see you know your way around a Maryland Blue Crab. Enjoy."

You could hear the combined sigh of relief from Arthur, Keith, Helen, and Angie. A scene had been avoided. Dinner was not ruined—yet.

Emily and Melinda exchanged glances. They would be extra careful with their conversation during dinner.

After extracting all the possible meat from between the thin white chambers of the crab, Mr. Skinnard showed the table how to use the mallet to break open the claw and pull out the meat hiding there.

Melinda murmured to Elvis that the crab, as delicious as it was, almost wasn't worth all the work. Mr. Skinnard frowned, but Melinda didn't know if he had overheard her or was reacting to a small cut on his finger that was exacerbated by the Old Bay Seasoning.

"Let me pour some water on that, Dad," Keith said. He angled his father's finger over the plate of crab debris and poured water from his glass over the tiny cut. He then dabbed the cut carefully with a clean napkin.

Mr. Skinnard is quite the king of his castle, with all his minions bowing and scraping to keep him happy, Emily thought, trying hard not to crack a smile. *The tension at the table is so high you'd think brain surgery was being performed rather than taking apart a crab.*

Thankfully, their waiter had impeccable timing. No sooner were the crab shells whisked away, than dinner plates arrived, for which Angie and Bob were most grateful. They had eaten only a roll and butter, so far, to stave off their hunger.

During the chatter accompanying the arrival of food, Emily leaned into Bob and whispered, "Lucky everyone knows how to eat an Irish stew and enjoy a chicken wing. No need for Mr. Skinnard to give instructions!" They both smiled.

Elvis made a toast, and for fifteen minutes, everyone was glad simply to enjoy their food.

"I'm loving these crab cakes," Keith said, finally breaking the silence. "How's your Bangers and Mash, Bob?"

"Delicious," he answered.

Everyone at the table stopped to look at the sausages and mashed potatoes on his plate covered with a pale, speckled gravy. Noticing their quizzical looks he added, "That's an onion gravy they're smothered in. Quite good, but I can feel my arteries hardening as we speak. Who wants to try some?"

He held his plate up, but everyone shook their heads.

Then, unexpectedly, Mr. Skinnard spoke up. "I will," he said. "Put some sausage and gravy on one of those bread and butter plates. I don't want any potatoes."

Bob quickly cut him an inch-thick piece of sausage and placed it on a small plate. Then he spooned some gravy over it and handed it down the table to Mr. Skinnard. Again, the siblings went quiet to await his reaction.

Emily wondered what it had been like to grow up in their household. They must have walked on eggshells the whole time, always worrying about doing the slightest thing that would set off their father's temper.

Mr. Skinnard cut the piece of sausage in half and put it in his mouth. No one breathed as he chewed then swallowed.

At last, he smiled.

"Excellent," he said. Everyone breathed out.

"Would you like some more?" Bob offered.

"No, that's enough. Thank you."

"You're most welcome," Bob replied, and everyone at the table relaxed and went back to enjoying their dinner.

After a few minutes, Mr. Skinnard raised his head and said, "I thought I saw a car like my old Buick Super Sport in the parking lot. Whatever happened to it after I sold it to you, Helen?"

No, no, no, Helen thought. *Here we go again.*

"It died back in 1988. You know that. Down in Dewey Beach. The engine just gave out. We had to have it towed, and it cost more to fix than the car was worth. That was thirteen years ago."

"That car was only eight years old at the time. How could the engine have been ruined so fast? It was that husband of yours. He didn't know how to take care of a car."

"I don't know what to say to you, Dad. I only know what the mechanic said. I thought Lesley took good care of the car. He had tune-ups done and the oil changed regularly."

"Those aluminum engines didn't last long," Arthur said in her defense.

"Your husband was a bum anyway," Mr. Skinnard added.

"Please, Dad. Could you not insult him to my face? I loved him, and he's the father of your grandchildren."

"Well, you made a poor choice for a husband. He couldn't support his family, and now he's left you."

"That's cruel, Dad," Angie said. "I was divorced before I met Ted. Don't blame Helen."

"Just saying," Mr. Skinnard said, then he tore off a piece of roll and dipped it into his stew.

Everyone was silent, hoping this was the end of the matter. They kept their eyes on their plates, avoiding any gesture that might start Mr. Skinnard off on another complaint.

Toward the end of the meal, Emily excused herself to use the ladies' room. After looking around quickly, she found a driftwood sign over the doorway to the foyer with the word Restrooms burnt into it. She followed the sign out to where they had come in and noticed a hallway with two doors. As she started down the hallway, she glanced into the separate room that was used for the bar and, there, perched on a stool watching TV was Mervin Crippens. His hair looked recently shampooed and his shirt was freshly ironed, but even cleaned up, he gave Emily an uneasy feeling. What was he doing here? Was he following the Skinnards? She had no way of knowing. She continued down the hall and found the ladies' room.

When she returned to the table she wanted to tell Bob about her sighting, but the men were embroiled in a discussion of deep-sea fishing.

Keith said, "Arthur and I are going deep-sea fishing on Thursday. I have a friend that keeps a boat here in Lewes, and he's taking some folks out. Maybe Bob and Elvis would like to join us. What do you say?"

Bob and Elvis looked at each other. Elvis smiled, raising his eyebrows in a gesture that conveyed "Why not?"

"We'd love to," Bob replied, then suddenly frowned and looked at Emily. Should he have checked with her first? He added, "That is, if the girls don't have anything planned."

Arthur shot a look at Keith that clearly said "Pussies."

Everyone at the table could read that look.

Emily hastily said, "No problem. You guys should go. Sounds like fun."

Elvis said, "Then it's a plan. What time do we leave?"

"Can you be ready at 7 a.m.?"

"Of course," Elvis replied, and Bob nodded in agreement.

"Glad to have you along," Arthur said.

"And Emily and Melinda can come over for lunch," Helen suggested. "Would you like to do that?"

"Definitely," Emily replied, seeing this as another chance to get to know the sisters better. "What time?"

"Come over at one. That's when Dad likes to eat lunch."

"Wonderful!" Melinda chimed in. "It'll be fun."

As they finished up their dinner, Mr. Skinnard asked if anyone was interested in dessert. The four from next door knew the routine now; they waited for the Skinnards to negotiate with their father.

"I don't know, Dad," Helen said. "Would you like some dessert?"

"Maybe just a piece of pie and a cup of coffee," he said.

The waiter appeared. Mr. Skinnard ordered a slice of apple pie, as did Arthur and Keith, while Helen and Angie decided to split a piece of cheesecake. Elvis and Melinda chose to share a rice pudding. Emily and Bob opted to split apple pie with ice cream. Only Mr. Skinnard chose coffee; everyone else stayed with water.

When the check came, Mr. Skinnard insisted on paying for everyone. Bob and Elvis protested in vain.

"It's one of the few pleasures of an old man," Mr. Skinnard argued. He finally agreed to let Bob and Elvis leave the tip.

As they were leaving, Bob found himself at the end of the entourage, accompanying Keith who was pushing his father's wheelchair down the ramp from the restaurant and into the parking lot. As he said his good-byes to the family and said a final thank you to Mr. Skinnard, the old man grabbed Bob's hand.

"I recognize you from the bookstore, young fella. Aren't you a lawyer?" he asked him.

"No, sir," Bob replied.

"You look just like that D.A. in Georgetown," Mr. Skinnard continued. "Are you following me?"

"No, sir, I'm not."

"Well, I just want to tell you—for the record—I did not have sex with that girl."

Bob looked at Keith, who had halted the wheelchair when he saw that his father was speaking earnestly to Bob.

"Sir, I don't know anything about that," Bob assured him and glanced again at Keith for an explanation.

Keith shrugged his shoulders.

"Well, maybe you do know, and maybe you don't, and maybe you were sent here to spy on me, but I did not harm that girl. You understand?"

"Yes, sir. I understand," Bob replied.

"Good. Just so we got that straight." Then he let go of Bob's hand and turned away from him, indicating the conversation was over.

"Just ignore him," Keith said softly to Bob. "That's what we do."

Emily walked over to where Keith and Bob were standing. She lowered her voice so Mr. Skinnard wouldn't hear, "Guys, I just saw that Mervin person in the bar."

"I saw him in the bookstore talking to your father," Bob added.

"It's really none of our business," Emily said. "But I just wanted you to know."

"I don't know why he's hanging around," Keith said. "But thanks for letting me know. Gotta catch up with the others."

"Okay," said Bob. "See you around."

That night as they were getting ready for bed, Bob remarked to Emily, "That old man is sure a stickler for doing things right."

"Well, he certainly opened my eyes," she replied.

"Really!" he responded. He turned around to face her, a bit surprised by her comment.

"Yes, and let me help you with that shirt. I think you're taking it off all wrong."

Catching her drift, he replied, "Yes, I think I need lessons in quite a few things."

Later, Emily awoke and glanced at the digital clock to see that it was almost midnight. She was still tired and didn't feel like getting out of bed, but she knew that, after only a few hours' sleep, she was unlikely to fall back to sleep again. She stayed in bed because she didn't want to disturb Bob, or possibly the others as she bumped her way around an unfamiliar house in the dark. Doors squeaked and boards creaked with alarming decibels in the still of the night.

When she woke early in her own home, she would get up and fix a bowl of cereal or do a crossword puzzle to pass the time. Lying next to Bob, she felt the constraints of being a couple, the sacrifices a partner makes to preserve the goodwill of the other. She also knew from her married days that such sacrifices can accumulate over time like mildewed leaves and neglected mulch, smothering the garden and poisoning the ground.

With the warmth of each embrace, a love affair becomes a living thing unto itself, with tendrils that wind within each other's psyche, offering the warmth of love in exchange for the limitations of movement—here, quite literally.

Emily lay, listening to Bob's breath, a soft rumbling sound in the dark. But simply lying there, Emily felt pleasure from feeling the warmth of his body beside her. She sighed and rolled on her side, hoping to go back to sleep.

But her thoughts would not be soothed away. How easy to become entrapped only to find your chosen one eventually forgetting his new lover reticence and letting fly an unkind word or disparaging look that snips off another blossom in your tree of love. After years of such bombardment, you find the tree withered and dead.

Could Bob become such a man as Richard Skinnard? Could his attention to neatness and detail, a virtue at the moment, turn over time into pettiness and cruelty?

Emily sighed anew, turned over on her other side, and sought sleep again. This time with some success.

TUESDAY

CHAPTER EIGHT
THE RING

Flashing lights woke Melinda at 3 a.m. She slowly swam up from the depths of sleep to see rotating bursts of red coming through an opening in the curtains. She shook Elvis until he awoke.

"Something's happening next door," she said as he slowly came out of oblivion. Only when she saw him open his eyes, did she swing her feet out of bed and pad on bare feet to the window.

"There's an ambulance and a police car outside. Must be for one of the Skinnards," she added as Elvis joined her. "I better go wake Emily and Bob. They'll want to see for themselves."

Elvis nodded, still too foggy to speak.

Melinda knocked gently on Bob and Emily's bedroom door. No answer. She knocked harder.

Only then did Bob call out, "Come in. We're awake now."

Melinda found them sitting up in bed, with looks of bewilderment on their faces.

"There's an ambulance and a police car next door."

"Oh no," Emily replied, gingerly searching with her bare feet for the floor and her slippers.

Bob was up quickly. "I want to see" was all he said as he followed Melinda back to her room.

Emily was right behind him.

Elvis had pulled back the curtains for a wider view.

"Has anything happened since I left?" Melinda asked.

"No," Elvis replied.

"Can you tell if there's anyone in the ambulance?" Emily asked.

"I don't think so. But you'll notice all the lights are on in the house. I wonder who the ambulance is for?"

At that moment, the front door of Chalet House opened, and the four could see two EMTs with a stretcher carefully carrying it through the doorway. There was someone underneath the blanket. From where the four watched, they couldn't decipher who it was. As the EMTs proceeded to the ambulance, Arthur and Keith appeared, dressed in bathrobes.

"Must be the old man," Elvis said sadly, referring to the figure on the stretcher.

As he spoke, the stretcher was loaded into the ambulance and its door slammed shut.

"See if you can quietly open the window," Emily urged. "I want to hear what they're saying."

Elvis ever so gently pressed against the sash and was able to raise it a few inches without a sound.

Keith appeared to say something to the EMTs as they got into their vehicle, but the four listening couldn't hear what it was. Keith then turned to his brother, but again they couldn't hear their words.

The ambulance slowly backed out of the driveway, lights still flashing but with no siren. Keith got in his Volvo and pulled out of the driveway. Arthur stood in the doorway and watched him drive away.

"Is it the old man?" Emily asked. "Do you think he's dead?"

"That would be my guess," Elvis replied.

"Melinda, could you tell?" Emily turned to her friend.

"No. Sorry."

"I'm tired," Bob said. "Let's go back to bed. Maybe we'll learn more in the morning."

They all nodded, and Bob and Emily returned to their room.

"Can you really go back to sleep after what we just saw?" Emily asked him.

"Watch me," he said. "One of my life skills."

Emily lay awake thinking, as she watched Bob tuck his arms under his head and slide into slumber. In no time, he was snoring softly. *If that was Mr. Skinnard on the stretcher, where were Helen and Angie?*

The four awoke later to gray skies that threatened rain. As they sat sipping coffee, they discussed the events of the previous night. They got no further than they had earlier. They tried to think of an excuse for one of them to call the Beebe Medical Center and ask about Mr. Skinnard, but given current privacy laws, they couldn't come up with a plan.

"Let's just forget about it for now," Elvis finally said. "If someone did die, I'm sure we'll see one of the family outside, and we can discreetly ask if everyone is alright. Now let's find something to keep us busy. Let's go somewhere."

"Suppose someone was murdered, like Angie predicted," Emily insisted. "Do you think we should tell the police about it?"

"No, we've no proof. We'd only look foolish." Bob replied.

"You're probably right. I need to stop worrying. How about Lewes again? Have any of you been there to stroll around?"

"Certainly not me," Melinda replied.

"Maybe years ago," Elvis said. "I think I went antiquing there with a previous girlfriend. Many, many years ago," he added with a nudge to Melinda. "The shops are probably all different now."

"How about you, Bob?"

"My ex and I went there a few times. We walked in and out of some stores. I don't remember much about them except for an ice cream shop where, after a dutiful half hour or so, I would beg to be allowed to wait for her."

"Well, are you all interested in going? You'll see some lovely old Victorian homes driving into Lewes. We could also go to the Zwaanendael Museum, which has exhibits honoring the first Dutch settlers of Sussex County. And on the way out, we can stop by this awesome bakery I know of to get a few tasty things for tonight and tomorrow."

"I'm all for shopping," said Melinda. "Not too keen on the museum. But I'll go if everyone else wants to."

"I think browsing the stores is all I'm interested in. Let's save the museum for another time," Bob said.

Elvis nodded agreement.

"Then it's settled," said Bob. "Let's go to Lewes."

A half hour later, Emily, Melinda, and Bob were seated in the living room waiting on Elvis.

"Do you know where he is?" Emily asked Melinda.

"I thought he was around here somewhere," she replied. "But he's not in the bedroom or bathroom or down here."

"Have you seen him, Bob?" Emily asked.

"No, sorry, I was too busy getting ready to go."

Minutes ticked by, and the three were getting restless.

"I'll look outside and see if he's doing something out there," Bob offered.

He went out and found Elvis cleaning out his car and shaking sand off the floor mats; a bottle of glass cleaner sat on the macadam.

"We were looking for you," Bob said. "We're all ready to go."

"Now?" Elvis asked him. "I still have to take a shower." He put the last floor mat back in the car and dusted his hands on his sweatpants.

"Well, the ladies are dressed and waiting. When did you think we were going?"

"I don't know. Sometime today."

Bob was uncomfortable. It had seemed straightforward to everyone else after their discussion that they would get ready to go. He frowned but didn't say anything. He didn't want to start an argument.

"Look, I can see you're upset with me," Elvis said as he started back toward the house, "but I guess I'm just used to going at my own pace."

"Did you see anyone from next door?" Bob asked, thinking Elvis might have had a reason for being outside.

"'Fraid not, but I wasn't looking." He entered the house with Bob right behind him.

Melinda took one look at him, still in his sweatpants. "I thought you were getting ready," she complained. "We've all been waiting for you."

"Sorry. I'll take a shower and be ready in fifteen."

He went upstairs, and Melinda looked at Emily.

"Sometimes Elvis can be very frustrating," Melinda said. She wasn't going to apologize for him. His behavior had nothing to do with her.

She did try to explain though. "Being self-employed, he's rarely on a schedule. I've gotten used to what he calls 'sidereal time,' which if you look it up—and I have—it isn't doing things on a whim. In astronomy, it has to do with telling time by the stars instead of the sun. I think it's just an excuse."

"Well, it's not the worst bad habit a person can have," Emily said, trying to comfort her friend.

"I'd have a tough time living with that," Bob commented softly.

Elvis was downstairs in ten minutes, showered, shaved, and dressed to go. He proposed that Bob drive again since Elvis still hadn't removed the umbrella and chairs from the RAV4.

The distance from Rehoboth to Lewes is only seven and a half miles, but the traffic on Route 1 was slow. It took them twenty minutes to get to Lewes, and a few more minutes to find a parking space.

The buildings and sidewalks were brick. Old-fashioned black steel lampposts lined the streets, and flags flew from each establishment. Shop windows were ablaze with fairy lights, and on the sidewalk, oak half-barrels spilled over with petunias and vinca vines.

With no particular goal in mind, they wandered in and out of a few shops that mingled antiques with used household goods. Down a side street, they spied an intriguing store with a large display window featuring hurricane lamps and porcelain washbasins.

"Let's go down here," Melinda pointed.

The store was set back from the street and accessible by six brick steps that led to a quaint brick patio. The heavy door was old wood below and thick glass above. Inside, the four found gleaming rolltop desks and all sizes of marble-topped tables. A glance at a few price tags let them know that everything was out of their price range.

Melinda wandered back into a dark corner, and they soon heard her "ooh" and "aah" over something she'd discovered. The other three followed and found her bent over a glass case of antique jewelry.

"Look at these rings, Elvis." She pointed to a collection of refurbished gemstones.

"I love this one." Her finger hovered over a small but brilliant ruby ring in a silver setting.

Noting their interest, the shop owner appeared behind the cabinet and unlocked it. He was an elderly man with pink cheeks and a full stomach over which a green velvet vest was tightly buttoned. He removed the ring and handed it to Melinda.

"That," he said, "is an unusual ring. It's a recycled palladium and vintage ruby engagement ring."

"I've never heard of a metal called palladium," Bob said.

"It's a rare, silvery-white metal discovered in 1803 by William Wollaston. I forget all the details now, but its name has something to do with the goddess Athena. Anyway, let me point out the three diamond baguettes on either side and the scrollwork below them. It's truly a unique ring."

Melinda held it up to the light and watched the ruby come alive with flashes of scarlet and magenta. She was dying to put it on her finger but thought that would look too much like she was hinting for a gift. Elvis was such a generous soul that he might feel compelled to sneak back and buy it for her.

"Do you know who it was made for?" Emily asked.

"I'm afraid not. It came with other jewelry that we purchased as a lot from an estate sale. I don't think the heirs had any idea of the value of this ring. They should have had it appraised."

Melinda got the hint that the ring was probably a costly item; it didn't have a price tag. She inwardly sighed and accepted this as an example of the old saying "If you have to ask, you probably can't afford it." She handed the ring back to the shop owner. "Thank you so much for taking this out of the case and showing it to me, but I don't think I can consider it today."

Emily noticed Bob and Elvis exchanging glances behind Melinda's back, but who knew what the price of that ring might be. If it was fifteen or twenty thousand dollars, that was probably more than even Elvis could afford.

"It was a pleasure to show it to you," the owner said, replacing the ring and locking up the cabinet.

"That's a gorgeous ring," Emily commented. "I'm fascinated by the brilliance of the ruby and the arcane scrollwork on the side of the ring. I can just picture it being worn by a Scottish princess with flowing red hair imprisoned in a tower by her lover's enemies."

"I'll bet it even has magical powers," Elvis said, encouraging her. "She rubs it three times, and a mist appears on the battlefield, creating a force field around her warrior prince that protects him from the swords of the enemy army."

"Ensuring the safe return of her lover and his freeing her from the tower in which she's been imprisoned," Emily concluded.

"Be quiet, you two," Bob warned, smiling. "You're attracting a crowd."

Indeed, a few customers had begun to gather around them to listen to their story.

Melinda didn't want to give Elvis any more encouragement. She decided to distract the others with her usual complaint, "I'm hungry. Let's find someplace for lunch." They all thanked the shop owner again and trooped outside.

"That was fun," Emily said. "Where shall we eat?"

CHAPTER NINE

THE HAIRY CLAW

They looked around and found a cozy bar at the end of a side street sitting right on the banks of the Lewes-Rehoboth Canal. Within minutes they were ensconced in a comfy booth wrapped in cool darkness, the guys with mugs of Guinness and the women with glasses of iced tea.

As they waited for their sandwiches, their view of the canal and its activity added surprising entertainment: boats were coming in from and heading out to the Delaware Bay. Some were fishing vessels, and some were pleasure boats. All were captained by tanned individuals who studiously kept to the rules of navigating the narrow canal.

The sailboats were the most mesmerizing. Their sails were broad expanses of white, blue, yellow, orange, and vibrant combinations thereof. They appeared in the window long enough to dazzle viewers and then floated away.

"Did you ever own a boat, Elvis?" Melinda asked.

"No, it didn't appeal to me," he said. "Too much work. I had a friend with one, and he spent every weekend scraping, painting, or doing one repair or other when he wasn't sailing. His wife hated that boat. They eventually divorced."

Sandwiches arrived, masterpieces of roast beef or ham and cheese sitting six inches high with pickles and chips.

Eyeing her sandwich, Emily mumbled, "I'll be taking half of mine home."

"I heard that," said Bob. "Sounds like a good midnight snack for me."

When they had finished eating, they filled up take-home containers with the leftovers and paid the bill.

Emily reminded them about stopping at a bakery on the outskirts of Lewes on their way home. "We can get some rolls for dinner, some Danish for breakfast tomorrow, maybe some cookies..."

"Yes, cookies," Melinda interrupted."

"And I thought we'd get something for our neighbors to thank them for treating us to dinner. It would also be a great excuse to knock on their door and, hopefully, get invited in. We can ask how their father is and, maybe, they'll tell us what happened last night."

"Good idea," said Melinda. "I want to check them out some more."

The guys agreed Emily's idea was a good plan.

They gathered up their leftovers bags and found Bob's car just as a few raindrops began to hit the brick sidewalk.

"Great timing," Bob said. "I hate to get wet."

The bakery was minutes away, and luckily, the rain was still just a drizzle as they dashed from the SUV to the bakery. Even with the rain, they could smell a heady aroma of yeasty pleasure.

Inside, there were few patrons. The four went from glass case to glass case admiring not only the usual cakes, pies, and cookies but also breakfast items, including four-inch-high sticky buns piled up with walnuts. The raisins and pecan cinnamon rolls with white icing promised to melt in your mouth.

"How will we decide?" Emily said to Bob.

"I love those donuts with chocolate icing," said Elvis pointing out a tray on the top shelf of a third case off to the side.

"Or what about those croissants?" said Bob, finding a fourth display case with rolls and loaves of French bread.

Fifteen more minutes passed before they narrowed down their purchases to a square of sticky buns, a dozen donuts, a box of cookies, a loaf of French bread, and an extra loaf of bread for their neighbors.

"As soon as we get home, I'm having a donut," Melinda said.

"Why not have one now?" Elvis said, and he began to open the bag.

"Not in my brand-new car," chided Bob, half-jokingly.

"Yes, sir," laughed Melinda. "I think I can make it home without one."

Shortly after they pulled into their driveway, Emily and Melinda knocked on their neighbors' door with baked goods in hand. The door was opened quickly by Keith and Angie, both laughing.

"Glad to see everyone so upbeat," Emily commented. She was hesitant to mention what they had seen the night before. It felt like prying. "We've just been to the bakery in Lewes and hoped you'd take some of the surplus off our hands. How 'bout it?"

Keith and Angie stood back to let them enter.

"Well, I think you could twist our arms," Keith said. "We usually plan a trip there ourselves, but we hadn't got around to it yet."

"Yes," said Angie, "And don't mind our laughter. Keith and I were just remembering a childhood trauma of mine that happened right here in this house during one of our vacations."

As Emily deposited the bag of bread and a paper plate of cookies on their dining room table she asked, "How is everyone today?"

Keith and Angie lost their smiles.

"Our father died last night," Keith said. "We're not sure if it was a heart attack or a stroke. Someone at the hospital will let us know."

"I'm so sorry," Emily said. "He looked to be in good health."

"Oh, he was, for the most part," Angie said, now looking down at the floor. "But he was in his nineties. He had a long life."

"I guess you'll be going home now?" Melinda asked.

"We're having his body sent up to Dover," Keith told them. "Arthur's wife will handle arrangements there. Until all the details of our father's death are cleared up, the police have asked the four of us to stay here. We can have the funeral next week. No hurry."

"Besides, the weatherman is predicting that the hurricane will hit Friday or Saturday," Angie added. "We want to be here to report any damage."

"Or hairy claws," Keith said, suddenly smiling and jostling Angie with his elbow.

"Hairy claws?" asked Emily, intrigued. "Are there wild animals around here?"

She was also wondering if Melinda was seeing Keith and Angie as adults or children. Melinda wasn't giving away any clues.

"That sounds like a good story. Can you share?" Emily pressed them.

Keith said, "It's what we were laughing about when you knocked on the door. You see, when we were children and used to stay here in the summer, my parents often went out to play cards with different friends they had here. Arthur and Frank, being older than me, usually had plans of their own to go to a dance or hang out with older teenagers. I always got stuck babysitting the girls."

He made a face, like one makes when saddled with a responsibility one used to hate but has made peace with over the years.

"Helen," he said, "was never a problem. She was the quiet one."

"Shut up," interjected Angie. "I'm just assertive."

"Where *is* Helen?" Emily asked. "And Arthur?"

"Helen and Arthur are at the grocery store," Angie responded.

Keith poked her. "Let me finish my story." He continued, "It happened right here, in this house, one summer vacation when the girls were still little. It was a dark, windy night, and the trees were making a lot of noise outside. It was kind of creepy, I'll admit. Helen had her own room, and Angie slept on a cot in Mom and Dad's room 'cause she was the youngest, maybe five years old. Anyway, the girls went to bed, and I was up watching TV when suddenly Angie started screaming. I went running upstairs and into her room. She was crying hysterically and told me that there was a hairy claw underneath her bed."

Angie started laughing again. "There *was*. To this day, I will swear that as I climbed into bed, a hairy claw came out from under the bed and grabbed my ankle!"

"How far out did it come?" Emily asked.

"Not far," Angie replied. "Maybe twelve inches or so, just enough to reach up and grab my ankle."

"Of course, it was a *foot* long," Keith chortled. "It was a *paw!*" And he started laughing again.

"I felt it," Angie insisted.

"Well, it doesn't matter now," Keith said. "What matters is that I was a good older brother and stayed with you until you went to sleep."

"Did it ever happen again?" Melinda asked.

"No," Angie replied. "Thank goodness."

"Did you tell your parents?" Emily asked.

"Oh no. We wouldn't bother them with it. But I did tell Arthur when he got home," Keith said, "and he got angry with Angie."

"He said I was imagining things, and that was wrong." Angie sounded hurt.

"No sympathy there," Emily commented.

"Well, I believed her," Keith said.

"You used to be nice to me when I was little," Angie reflected. "But you were mean when I got older."

"You wouldn't listen to me. You and Helen both. If you'd just worn some makeup, and had your hair done differently, you could have gotten a very successful man to marry you. I mean, your second husband turned out to be all right, but poor Helen is floundering around dating losers just like her ex. I don't understand her."

"Maybe it's not worth the effort to pretend to be somebody you're not," Angie said. "Helen likes who she is. She doesn't want to spend her whole life trying to please some rich dude. We had to do enough pretending when we were around Dad. Give her a break."

"If you say so," Keith replied. "But if she would just fix herself up more, her life could be so different."

"Brothers are such a pain," Angie sighed, sounding like a teenager.

"Sometimes we're useful too," Keith said. "Helen's not here to tell you, but I did stop her once from walking out in front of a speeding car on our way to school."

"I guess," Angie agreed. "And I remember that time Arthur rescued her when bees swarmed her in the backyard."

"Well, we'd better go," Emily interrupted, uncomfortable at being an outsider hearing all these family reminiscences.

"And thank you for the bread and cookies," Angie said, walking them to the door. "But it wasn't necessary."

"Yes, it was," Melinda said and hugged her. She could see how much Angie needed it. Melinda thought, *Angie and Helen have spent their whole lives trying to please others. It must be quite a burden.*

"Will we still see you on Thursday for lunch?" Angie reminded them.

"We'll be here. Give our love to Helen and Arthur," Emily added as they left.

"Will do," Angie said.

As they neared Suits Us, Emily asked Melinda, "Did you see Angie and Keith as adults or children?"

"They were older than the last time, teenagers I'd say. Their father's death has aged them."

"Interesting. I wonder what they'll look like on Thursday."

WEDNESDAY

CHAPTER TEN
ABBEY ROAD

Wednesday morning was sunny but cooler. The house next door had been quiet the night before, and the four friends enjoyed a night of uninterrupted sleep until a knock at the door woke Emily at 8 a.m. She put on a robe, left Bob sleeping, and went downstairs to answer the door.

Two police officers stood there. Surprised, Emily let them in.

They introduced themselves as Officers Randall Smith and Janice Reston.

"We just have a few questions about what happened Monday night. You are aware that Mr. Skinnard, who was staying next door with his children, died that night?" Officer Reston asked.

"We know," Emily said. "We saw the ambulance and someone being taken away, and yesterday, his children told us he was dead."

"The death has been temporarily labeled as suspicious, so we're doing an investigation. We'd like to speak to you and your housemates about it."

"Let me wake them up," Emily said. "Please have a seat."

The officers looked around and settled into the easy chairs in the living room.

Emily went upstairs to Bob first.

Giving him a hard shake to wake him up, she said softly, "The police are downstairs. You better get dressed and come down."

"Okay," he replied groggily. Emily hastily shed her nightgown and robe and put on a sweatshirt and jeans. Then she went to the other bedroom and found Melinda and Elvis already up and dressing.

"We heard you talking downstairs," Melinda said. "We'll be right there."

Emily returned to the officers and asked, "Do you mind if I make some coffee? We're all pretty sleepy."

"No problem," Officer Reston replied. "We'll have some too."

Emily went to the kitchen and quickly started the coffeemaker. She found six clean mugs in the dishwasher and arranged them on a tray with spoons, the sugar bowl, and the nondairy creamer. She tidied up the kitchen while the coffee dripped through, and as soon as it was ready, she poured out six cups and took the tray into the living room.

By this time, the other three had come downstairs and were all crowded onto the sofa. Emily put her tray down on the coffee table and pulled a chair over from the dining room.

"Okay?" she asked.

The officers nodded and helped themselves to coffee.

She noticed that while she had been in the kitchen, the officers had set up a small tape recorder on the coffee table.

When everyone had a hot mug in hand, Officer Smith punched the Record button and said, "Wednesday, August 29, 2001, 8:17 a.m. Investigation into the death of Richard J. Skinnard. Everyone, please state their name for the record." He nodded to them, and they began:

"Emily Menotti."

"Robert Bowie."

"Melinda Allende."

"Elvis Gdanski."

"Let's start with you, Emily," Officer Reston said. "What do you recall of the events of Monday night, August 27?"

"There's not much to tell," she began. "We were woken up by flashing lights next door. We looked out of the bedroom window. We saw someone carried out on a stretcher. That's it."

The other three nodded in agreement.

"Had you spoken to your neighbors previously? Did they talk about their father's health?"

"We've all spoken to them," Bob answered. "We had dinner with them on Monday night at Irish Airs in Lewes. But there was no specific talk about their father's health. We could all see that he was very old and sometimes needed a wheelchair."

"Was there any animosity expressed by the children to their father? Did you ever get the feeling that he was in danger?" Officer Smith asked.

The four were surprised by these questions; they all sat up straighter. They looked at each other. Did the police think he'd been murdered?

"No," answered Emily. "He seemed to be a difficult man to get along with, but there were no specific incidents of animosity."

"Until we get the final word from the coroner," Officer Smith said, "we are treating this as a suspicious death. That's why we're questioning you."

"Suspicious?" Elvis said. "He was in his nineties. I would think he died of natural causes."

"I can't tell you anything other than we found something at the scene that is causing us to look at this as a possible homicide. Anything you can tell us about the family would be helpful."

"Nothing that we know of," Emily answered and looked around at her friends.

They all shook their heads in agreement.

"We only just met them on Sunday," she added.

"Interview terminated at 8:43 a.m.," Officer Reston announced and pushed the Stop button on the recorder. "Thank you for your time," she added. She pocketed the recorder, and both officers stood up.

The four friends stood up also, and Emily accompanied the officers to the door.

"If you think of anything else, please give us a call," Officer Smith said while handing Emily a business card. "Both my work and home numbers are there. Call anytime."

The officers left, and Emily shut the door behind them.

"We've got a murder, my friends. What are we going to do about it?" She came back to the living room and sat in one of the now-empty easy chairs.

"I don't know what we *can* do," Bob said.

"We can ask questions," Melinda said, smiling. "Emily and I are good at that. But not right now, I need some breakfast."

"Can't sleuth on an empty stomach," Emily agreed. "Let's get out those sticky buns from the bakery."

"Well, there's not much we can do this morning," Bob concluded. "Our neighbors will be busy talking to the police themselves, as well as making arrangements for their father. I think we have to hold off our investigation until things settle down next door."

"Then what shall we do today?" Elvis asked, coffee in one hand

and sticky bun in the other. "I believe I've got a sugar high going nicely. Let's do something that involves walking."

"I agree. I can't think of any way to learn more about what happened to Mr. Skinnard right now. We'll just have to wait for an opportunity to speak to the kids again. How about a trip to Ocean City?" Emily suggested. "They've got a lengthy boardwalk. That should tire you out."

"And how about you drive, Elvis?" Bob added. "I don't want my car getting dinged up in that huge parking lot at the end of Ocean Highway."

"No problem, old man. Like I said, I've got the heebie-jeebies already."

Emily saw Bob grimace at being called an old man, but he let it go. The four had been living together for four days now. Both she and Bob were used to living by themselves, and she had to admit that she missed her "alone" time. Bob was probably feeling the same way.

Melinda was sitting quietly and taking note of the conversation and interactions. This was a side to Elvis she hadn't seen before; he was usually relaxed and unhurried. She was also thinking, like Emily, that the lack of privacy was beginning to wear on her. It would be nice to spend an hour soaking in the tub with a good book. However, there was only one bathroom in the rental home. She wouldn't have minded staying back by herself, but Elvis would probably want to stay with her. There was no nice way she could extricate herself from their plans.

"I'm all for going to Ocean City," she finally spoke up. "What does it have, besides a long boardwalk, that makes it an attractive destination? Won't it just be more souvenir shops and more ice cream stands?"

"On the boardwalk, there's this wild art gallery that's two stories tall," Emily told her. "It's crammed with hundreds, maybe thousands of affordable paintings that go from hideous to gorgeous. There's landscapes, portraits, and weird modern art pieces. You wander through and look at them all and see if there isn't something that appeals to you. I love it. I challenge you to go there and not buy something."

"I like Ocean City for their restaurants," Bob picked up from Emily. "Most people will tell you that Phillips Crab House is the best, but I prefer Thompson's, that is, if it's still there. I think their crab cakes are the best I've ever eaten."

"If you want to dance, even in the middle of the afternoon, there's a place called Seacrets, on the bayside," Emily offered. "Music is always playing. You can drink, dance, wade in the water. They have it all."

"What about Fager's Island?" Bob said. "I had their bacon-wrapped shrimp one time, and it melted in my mouth. I love that place."

Emily added, "And you can dance there too. If you stay after dinner until the band starts, you can dance all night, and then go out to the deck and sit under the stars. It's my favorite place in Ocean City. When I'm feeling rich, that is. It's very expensive."

"You've sold me," Elvis said.

"I'm hungry again already," Melinda said. "Let's get ready and go."

Late Wednesday morning, the hour's drive to Ocean City, Maryland, was an easy one. There was little traffic in Rehoboth and few cars could be seen in Dewey Beach.

Driving south of Dewey Beach, Melinda pointed to a pair of concrete towers rising out of the oceanside dunes. "What are those?" she asked. "They look like something out of a science fiction movie."

The lower half of the sixty-foot towers had six narrow windows on two separate levels, while the upper half had two semicircular, horizontal windows only one foot tall. The roof of the structures was flat, encircled by a railing.

"That's Towers Beach, named for those towers," explained Elvis. "They were erected during World War II. They were built for observation, so soldiers could be on the lookout for German warships and U-boats."

"I'd love to go inside them," Bob said. "But I can see they're surrounded by wire fence."

"I would assume that they're Army property and no one's allowed in there," Elvis said. "There's ten or eleven of these towers up and down the Delaware coast," he added. "There's one in Lewes at Fort Miles that is open to the public now. I don't know about the others."

"Delaware was a target for the Germans," Bob explained, "because the Delaware River led to both the DuPont Chemical plant in Wilmington and the Philadelphia Shipyards."

"Thank you, Professor Bob."

They were now driving on the loneliest part of Route 1 with a view of grass-covered dunes rolling to the ocean on their left, and flat, marshy land on their right that led to Rehoboth Bay.

"Look at all this beautiful undeveloped land," Elvis commented. "If it hadn't been for former Governor Russell Peterson and the Delaware Coastal Zone Act of 1971, you'd be looking at a Shell Oil refinery."

"No way!" Melinda said. "How awful would that have been!"

"Yes, way," Elvis responded. "Everyone from the local Chamber of Commerce to members of Richard Nixon's cabinet battled against the Coastal Zone Act. Governor Peterson was a true conservative if you take that word to include conservation."

"I remember when he was governor," Bob said. "He was an unusual man. Besides being a politician, he was a scientist, a DuPonter, and a Republican, but he always put what was right over what was politically expedient."

"I believe the Coastal Zone Act is under constant attack by politicians and big business who only see this thriving ecosystem as a source of revenue," Emily commented.

"Every time I've ever driven down this road, I'm always afraid I'm going to see it has been taken over by big hotels and strip malls," Elvis sighed.

"I think a few home developers have chipped away at parts of it," Bob said. "But it looks like the Act is holding strong."

"Thank goodness," Emily replied.

Elvis continued with the travelogue. "I do believe we have now reached Bethany Beach, and if you blink your eyes, you will have missed it. Bethany Beach, my dear Melinda, is not known for anything except that the houses are built too close to the water and will be the first to go when global warming strikes in earnest. Now, as your chauffeur, let me point out that the next town of interest is Fenwick Island."

Elvis was being unusually chatty, and Emily glanced at Melinda, who shrugged her shoulders. Bob, sitting in the shotgun seat up front, didn't pick up on their concern.

Perhaps it was the caffeine, or maybe Elvis was also chafing under the lack of private time. Emily wondered if they should split up for a while on the boardwalk.

"How about if we give each other some space once we get to

Ocean City," she suggested. "We could each go our own way for an hour or two, or as couples, me and Bob, Melinda and Elvis. What do you think?"

"Or how about me and Emily and Bob and Melinda?" Elvis grinned.

Emily and Melinda exchanged glances.

"No offense, Melinda," Bob said, "But I was looking forward to some time alone with Emily."

"No offense taken," Melinda said, but there was a whinge in her voice that betrayed her hurt feelings at her company being scorned by both men.

"I was just joking," Elvis said with a bit of exasperation.

"It would be nice if Emily and I went off by ourselves for a while," Bob said again to make sure he was understood.

"What do you think, Melinda?" Elvis said. "Can you stand me for a while without your sidekick?"

"Of course! Let's wander about and get lost in a fun house or something." She could tell he was out of sorts, but even her clairsentience couldn't tell her why.

The last town in Delaware is Fenwick Island, whose homes and businesses blend seamlessly into the outskirts of Ocean City, Maryland.

Melinda glanced at a street sign. "One hundred and forty-third street! I guess this place is a little bigger than Rehoboth."

"And very different," Elvis responded. "Give it a few more blocks and you'll see the high-rise condos on the beach."

"There was a building boom here in the sixties and seventies," Bob added. "Friends of mine bought a two-story condo on ninety-ninth for about thirty-seven thousand dollars. Seemed like a lot of money at the time. Probably a great investment now. I imagine they make a fortune renting it out in the summer."

"Hate to be cynical, old pal," Elvis said. "But they're probably divorced by now and had to sell it and split the profits."

"Is this why you're not married?" Melinda asked. "Because you think all marriages end in divorce?"

"No, it's not why I'm not married, and let's not discuss this in front of others."

The temperature in the car dropped ten degrees.

"Look!—"Bob interjected to get their attention—"There's the building where my friends own a unit, the Ninety-Nine."

Out of the sand rose a twenty-story obelisk of black glass that acted as a photographic negative, reflecting the white sand and blue sky as black sand and gray sky.

"Looks gruesome from the outside," Emily said.

"My friends' two-story unit is on the eighteenth floor. The views are spectacular. You can look east out over the ocean, or west out over the bay, catching both sunrise and sunset."

There was notable silence from Elvis and Melinda as they continued driving down the Coastal Highway. After passing blocks upon blocks of impressive high-rises and the strip shopping centers built to service them, they arrived at the older section of Ocean City. The street was lined with two-story stucco condos, family restaurants, and a miniature golf course on every corner.

At the end of the road was the Hugh T. Cropper Inlet Parking Lot. On this serene summer day along the far side of the parking lot, you could see fishing boats and family yachts plying the inlet. After the car was parked, the four wandered silently down to the jetty and watched the boats for five minutes. Emily was concerned about her friends.

"Let's get going," Elvis finally said. "I can smell those French fries. How long is this boardwalk?"

"It's about a mile," Emily said. "Shall we eat lunch separately, then meet around two?"

"I like that idea," Bob said. "Where shall we meet?

"How about the Ocean Art Gallery?" Emily suggested. "It's easy to find. It's on the boardwalk at Second Street. Believe me, you absolutely can't miss it. It's covered with paintings, and the sign consists of three-foot-high orange letters saying 'Ocean Gallery.'"

"See you then," Elvis replied, and he and Melinda started in the direction of the boardwalk.

"I'm worried," Emily said.

"You worry too much," Bob replied and took her hand. "Let's find some coffee. I'm not very hungry. I think I could be happy with just a soft pretzel or ice cream cone for lunch. How about you?"

"Sounds good. We haven't had any time by ourselves so far on this vacation, except, of course, at bedtime. But I enjoy just being alone with you, either walking or sitting and talking."

"Me too," he replied, as they strolled hand in hand down the boards.

Eventually, they came to a candy store that sold coffee and baked goods as well.

"Let's stop in here and get coffee," Bob said.

They found a cozy booth of painted white wood with green seat cushions and starfish placemats. Photos of smiling people, who were probably the owners and their families, crowded the walls. The air was rich with the aroma of newly baked goods and the subtle scent of cinnamon.

"I'm suddenly hungry," Emily said. "I think I'll order one of those blueberry scones I see in that glass case over there."

A woman in faded jeans and a chef's apron appeared at their table.

"What can I get y'all?" she asked in a voice Emily recognized as Sussex County southern. She had a lazy smile and wavy grey tendrils of hair escaping from a bun atop her head.

"Coffee and a blueberry scone," Emily said.

"Just coffee for me," Bob added.

The waitress reached around a corner and produced two heavy brown mugs and a metal pot of coffee which she placed on their table. A small bowl of individual creamers and a container of sugar packets quickly followed. Before Emily finished pouring coffee for them both, their waitress returned with a scone and placed it in front of Emily.

"Y'all enjoy now," she advised them and turned to leave.

"Before you get your fingers all messy," Bob said when he was sure the waitress was out of earshot, "I have something for you."

From his pocket, he pulled out a small package wrapped in white paper tied up with a red ribbon. He laid it on the Formica tabletop and pushed it across to her.

Emily blushed. She wasn't prepared for gifts.

"You shouldn't have," her mouth said, but her grin said she was pleased he had.

"Open it," Bob urged her.

Emily pulled the ribbon off and unwrapped the small box within. She lifted the lid to find the silver shape of a small heart covered with tiny diamonds attached to a thin silver chain.

"I'm giving you my heart," Bob confessed across the table.

"This is why you went into that jewelry store on Rehoboth Avenue, isn't it?" Emily asked.

"Yes, you got me."

"Thank you, I love it," Emily said and lifted it from the box to watch the heart dangle from the chain and sparkle in the fluorescent light.

Bob took the necklace from her and got up. He gently placed the chain around Emily's neck, surprising even himself that his large hands could work the tiny latch to secure it. Then he kissed her lightly on the lips and sat back down.

"I love you," Emily said, only loud enough for Bob to hear.

He just smiled, took a sip of his coffee, and said, "I'll take some of that scone now."

"Of course," she said and cut it exactly in half.

A few minutes shy of 2 p.m., Emily and Bob made their way to the Ocean Gallery. There was no sign of their friends, so they entered from the boardwalk and slowly made their way down aisles of art of every size and genre. There were copies of grand masters as well as originals in oil, water, acrylic, and combinations that included fabric and jewels. There were four- and six-foot-high canvases contrasting with miniatures that had barely recognizable subjects. All were jumbled together, on top of each other, next to each other, around corners and under stairways. As Bob and Emily followed the aisle, it became a labyrinth that snaked back upon itself several times. They came to a staircase and went upstairs and found more paintings that they judged to be little different than what they had seen downstairs, but no Elvis or Melinda.

"See anything you like?" Emily asked Bob, trying to decide about a painting of a French cottage with a pretty garden that she didn't need but found appealing.

"No. This stuff is all too dusty anyway. I wouldn't want it in my house."

"Do you think they left?"

"I'm starting to hear their voices. Let's keep going."

The maze finally took them to a stairway that led down to Second Street. As they descended, they could see a cash register station and an impatient salesclerk holding a large painting. When they got to the bottom of the steps, they could hear Melinda and Elvis arguing.

"Now I have to ask *permission* before I buy something?"

It was Melinda's voice, loud, angry, injured.

"No, I don't mean that. But maybe you could consult me before you buy something to put on the wall in *my* house." Elvis was trying to sound reasonable, but it came out harsh.

"*Your* house! You told me to think of it as *our* house."

"Yes, it is, but this is a big picture, and we should discuss important purchases."

At the cash register station, Emily and Bob saw what "big" and "important" was: a thirty-by-forty-inch oil painting of the iconic Beatles' Abbey Road album cover showing John, Paul, George, and Ringo crossing the street. Paul's outfit, black suit and bare feet, had once sparked the infamous "Paul is Dead" rumor.

Melinda was holding a sales receipt, so the deed was done. Emily was picturing the painting in Elvis's living room, which he had decorated as an homage to Edgar Allan Poe with hurricane lamps, an old desk, and other Victorian-era artifacts. The painting would not work in there, nor in the dining room, bedrooms, and kitchen; all continued the Victorian theme. The couple had a problem.

"It's not going to fit in the car," Bob, ever the practical one, pointed out.

Melinda calmly turned to him and said, "I'm having it shipped."

"Let's take another walk," Emily said to Bob. And to Melinda and Elvis she said, "We'll be back in fifteen," and pulled Bob toward the boardwalk.

Melinda was steaming. She knew she was in the wrong, but not entirely. *Yes, I could have consulted Elvis. But I bought it on impulse because I love the Beatles and love that album.* Her thoughts continued to boil. *Why did Elvis have to get so huffy so quickly? Couldn't he have admired my purchase and then calmly discussed where to hang it?*

"Melinda, it's not about *your* house or *my* house," Elvis said, watching her face. "But can't you see that it just doesn't match the way I've decorated?"

"So, home décor is more important than I am?"

"Melinda, I know you're not this dumb."

"So now I'm dumb?" But she smiled. Elvis had painted himself into a corner.

He realized he was smarter than this too. This was the most lamebrain argument they had ever had, spouting clichés back and forth to each other. What was going on with them? They were both too savvy to be arguing like this.

Elvis saw her smile and burst out laughing. "I can't believe we are saying these things."

"Me neither," she said. "Can I keep the painting and we'll discuss it when we get home?"

"There's no asking. You bought a painting. It's yours. Congratulations."

"I love you." But Melinda understood how this first major argument had tarnished the innocence of their relationship.

Elvis felt it too.

"Something is brewing between those two and I don't know what it is," Emily said. "Did you notice it earlier?"

"You said Melinda has never been married before, right?"

"Yes."

"Has she ever been seriously in love?"

"Not that she's confided to me."

"Perhaps that's the problem. How old is she?"

"Thirty-eight."

"Love and entitlement are unsettling emotions for someone who's not used to them. You and I have been married and divorced. Maybe entertained a romance or two?" He raised his eyebrows with this question, hoping she would understand his affairs of the heart.

"Of course," Emily responded, remembering her boyfriend Bud.

"She's in unknown territory. Neither of us knows Elvis very well, except that he's never been married before either. They're both struggling with feelings we've already dealt with."

"It's like the mumps and the measles." Emily laughed at her analogy. "They hit you harder the older you are when you get them."

She grabbed his hand. "I'm glad you and I have already been exposed."

"Agreed." He squeezed her hand. "Let's give them five more minutes and head back."

They walked through another souvenir shop, looked at the racks of lewd tee shirts, turned their gaze in the opposite direction to the kids enjoying the surf, and then returned to the Ocean Gallery.

Elvis and Melinda, both smiling, were waiting for them.

Elvis said, "Are we ready to roll?"

"Was there somewhere else in OC you wanted to visit?" Elvis asked as he maneuvered the RAV4 out of the crowded parking lot.

"What would you say to a cocktail on the beach under waving palm trees and listening to the sound of island music? Or it might be reggae or rock 'n' roll," Emily asked.

"Anything alcoholic would be a blessing right now," Melinda sighed.

"Okay. Elvis, please drive to Forty-Ninth Street, and then we'll start looking for the parking lot. Do you know where we're going, Bob?"

"Seacrets. I think we have the perfect day for it if we can get in. Sometimes it's crowded."

"I'm hoping that, on a Wednesday afternoon, it won't be too busy yet."

They traveled through the oldest section of Ocean City. Here, five- and six-story hotels with crumbling concrete facades and peeling paint lined the streets. Stores spouted faded awnings and cardboard signage taped over grimy windows. Elvis followed the turns back up to the Coastal Highway, where modern hi-rise condominiums commanded the shorefront and sparkled with clean glass and steel beams. At Forty-Ninth Street, he found signs directing him to a parking lot for Seacrets. They were pleased to find plenty of open spots, which translated into lots of room inside.

As they were walking to the club, Melinda asked, "Tell me again, what's so special about Seacrets?"

Emily laughed. "If you want the island experience but don't care for ocean travel, Seacrets is the ideal substitute. When you walk through the wooden doors, you enter a world of Tiki bars, sand beaches, palm trees, colorful birds, and even chickens running loose. There are cozy tables under the palms, or lounge chairs on the beach, and floating rafts in the bay with waitresses who will wade out to take and deliver your order."

Melinda, intrigued, said, "Tell me more."

"Music is piped in everywhere but is occasionally broken up by live music down on the beach. People are dancing everywhere, swaying in bathing suits, long skirts, or surfer shorts. It's easy to forget you're on the mainland."

As they entered Seacrets, Melinda clapped her hands, imbibing the ambience. "Oh yes! Let's stay here for a while."

They found a table under some palms not far from the bay where most of the rafts were already filled with tan bikinied bodies gleaming in the sun.

Everywhere was color! Sparkling blue sky, emerald green leaves, the tan trunks of trees, a red parrot here, brown chickens there, yellow sun, pink tee shirts, bleached white hair—a kaleidoscope glittering in front of them as they sat and waited for their drinks.

"We didn't have much to eat on the boardwalk," Bob spoke up. "I'd like to order a sandwich."

"We didn't eat at all," Elvis said. "I've already picked out a crab cake platter with fries."

"Jerk chicken for me," Melinda said and winked at Elvis.

"Just regular grilled chicken for me," said Emily.

Twenty minutes later, the four had food and drinks, Melinda and Emily going "tropical" with huge Island Margaritas, and Bob and Elvis slaking their thirst with something called a Rum Runner.

"I wonder what our neighbors are doing today," Emily thought aloud. "I hope nobody has died while we're gone."

"Nothing we can do, honey," Bob assured her. "This is our vacation too. We can't plan our activities around what might happen next door to people we hardly know."

"You're right," she agreed and took another sip of her margarita. She was almost ashamed of how easy it was to dismiss the murder a distressed Angie had heralded their very first night.

"This is heaven," Emily chirped as the piped-in music changed from golden oldies to reggae.

The air temperature was in the low eighties and augmented by a soft breeze off the bay. The laughter of the folks on the rafts created a soft background patter, and the sun was still high enough not to be in their eyes. Their stomachs full and muscles and brains relaxed by drinks, they lolled in their cushioned chairs under the palms and could have fallen asleep.

"Emily!" Melinda suddenly shouted just as Emily was about to doze off. "Where did you get that stunning necklace? It's beautiful. How did I miss it earlier?"

"Bob gave it to me this morning when we stopped for coffee on the boardwalk."

Bob said nothing, only grinned.

"Good show, old man," said Elvis, then he took Melinda's hand. "Let's dance."

"Here?"

"Well, maybe over there where the other dancers are," he said, pointing to an area in the sand used as a dance floor.

"Okay."

With beaming smiles to Bob and Emily, they got up and left.

Emily looked over at Bob, thinking she would like to dance too. She was startled to see that he was fast asleep. She wouldn't wake him.

She looked over at Melinda and Elvis, arms around each other, swaying to a reggae tune she didn't recognize. She smiled and closed her eyes.

THURSDAY

CHAPTER ELEVEN

Family Stories

Thursday morning, the guys went deep-sea fishing. Arthur and Keith were gung-ho with the idea, and they had sold Elvis on it entirely. Bob was hesitant, but Elvis eventually convinced him.

"I'm surprised the police are allowing them to go, what with this investigation going on," Emily said.

"Maybe they just have to stay in the area, and I guess that includes Lewes," Bob said.

"I really don't care for those guys," he said to Elvis. "I need you as a buffer against them. I'd love to go fishing, but they're so uptight they'll take all the fun out of it."

"Have you ever been deep-sea fishing?" Emily asked Bob in their room while he dressed in his oldest jeans and sweatshirt.

Reaching for his waterproof jacket, Bob nodded. "Once, as a kid. I had a great time. My dad and uncles took me, and we ran into a school of bluefish. I caught thirty or forty of them. I was thrilled. I kept reeling them in, and I thought I was the best fisherman ever. Then we ate bluefish for the rest of the week. They were oily and smelly, and I hated the taste. If I catch any today, I'll throw them back."

"Don't let the other guys see you do it."

"Elvis won't mind."

"What about Arthur and Keith?"

"Can't say I care what they think."

As they walked downstairs he asked Emily, "What are you and Melinda up to?"

"This morning, I think we're just cleaning up the cottage and doing laundry. Then we're having lunch with Helen and Angie. I need to ask them some questions. I still haven't figured out Angie's outburst that first night we were here. How did she know if someone was really in danger of dying?"

"I've got your sandwiches packed," Melinda said as she and Elvis appeared out of the kitchen.

"I won, Mel," Elvis said.

"What did you win?" Bob asked.

"Our bet," Melinda said. "I said you would change your mind about going."

"I thought you were never wrong," Emily said.

"No one's infallible," she laughed, "and I'm glad."

The guys left with a joke or two about being lost at sea, leaving the cottage strangely quiet.

"It's spooky with them gone," Emily said. "There's an old folk song that goes 'In the pines, in the pines, where the sun never shines...' I forget what the story is, but I remember it being very sad."

"Oh, cheer up. Let's have a cup of coffee and another sticky bun. What would you like to do this morning that the guys never want to do?"

"A massage and a mani-pedi," Emily sighed.

"Rock on, Em! That's perfect. I'll call now. It's nine o'clock. They should be open."

Melinda made them both appointments for ten thirty.

"This is perfect," Emily said. "Lunch next door is at one. We'll be relaxed and beautiful for the start of our investigation."

By ten fifteen, dishes had been stashed in the dishwasher, a load of laundry had begun, showers had been taken, and Emily and Melinda were out the door. Within minutes they lay side-by-side on massage tables, listening to the soothing sounds of the ocean broadcast from the spa's stereo system as professional hands kneaded away the tension stored in their necks and shoulder muscles. Life seemed just about perfect.

"We need to do this again next year," Melinda purred contentedly.

"Agreed."

The fishing boat waiting for the two Skinnard men, along with Bob and Elvis, was christened the Sez Who? When the four got to the dock, half a dozen other men were waiting too. One of them was Mervin Crippens.

"Oh, jiminy," Arthur said to Keith. "What's he doing here?"

"We'll try to stay away from him," Keith replied.

"On this tiny boat?" Arthur laughed. "I doubt we'll be able to."

They never had a chance to avoid him. Mervin spied them

immediately and walked over. He was dressed in the same slovenly white shirt and polyester pants he'd worn when they first saw him on the boardwalk.

"Very sorry about your dad," he muttered, pulling out a pack of cigarettes and a Bic Lighter from his pants pocket.

Arthur and Keith murmured "Thank you" together and said nothing further.

"You know your dad owed me some money." Mervin said in a low voice to discourage anyone from overhearing. "Can you guys repay the two grand he owed me?" The lighter flared and Mervin lit his cigarette, cupping it in his hands to block the morning breeze.

"Dad never said anything to me about owing you money," Arthur nervously replied. He could see that the others in their fishing group had begun boarding the boat. "How do I know you're even telling the truth?"

"So you're not going to pay up?" Mervin asked, glancing up at Arthur over cigarette smoke.

"No," said Keith. "We don't trust you."

Mervin glared at Keith, then turned and started to walk away. It seemed he had changed his mind about going on the fishing excursion. Suddenly he stopped, turned around, and shouted back at Keith and Arthur, "I've got bad news for you boys. Your parents were never married to each other. You two and your silly little sisters are all bastards. How do you like that?" Then he turned back around and resumed walking.

"That's a lie," Arthur shouted after him.

"Don't bother us again," Keith added.

"Don't worry, I won't, you cheating bastards." Mervin hurried off.

Arthur and Keith looked at each other in shock.

"No way," said Keith.

"I believe him," Arthur replied. "It's just the sort of thing our father would do."

"Let's not tell Helen and Angie. They're already upset about Dad's death. No sense adding to their grief."

"Agreed."

Bob and Elvis had tried to stand out of earshot when Mervin had asked the Skinnard men for money, but they couldn't miss the words Mervin had loudly announced to anyone within twenty yards of him. They didn't say anything to the brothers who were now angry and silent.

As the four boarded the boat, Bob thought, *I hope the fishing's good. We'll need the distraction.*

At 12:55 p.m., Emily and Melinda knocked on their neighbors' door. Angie answered.

Emily presented her with more zinnias from the garden. Angie thanked her and put the flowers in a white vase and set it on the dark wood sideboard. The red and orange blooms brightened up the brooding atmosphere of Chalet House immediately.

Dishes of chicken salad, lettuce, tomato, fruit salad, and potato chips were already in the center of the table, along with a pitcher of lemonade.

"You're holding up well after losing your father," Emily said. "Have you been sleeping alright?"

"Not well, if I'm honest," Helen replied. "But I keep telling myself that he had ninety-eight good years."

"I don't think all ninety-eight of them were good," Angie said. "Remember he lived through the Great Depression."

"Did he fight in World War II?" asked Emily.

"No, he didn't," Helen said. "He had two small children when we entered the war. They didn't take young men with families. Not until the end. Then I think he was drafted, but the war was over before he had to fight."

"Lucky for you," Melinda remarked.

Helen and Angie exchanged looks that said *Maybe not.*

Emily changed the subject. "The food looks scrumptious!"

"And, as always, I'm starved," said Melinda.

"Let's eat," said Helen, and she and Angie sat down.

Lunch was pleasant. Helen entertained them with stories of when Rehoboth was originally a camp meeting place for the Methodists.

"I remember what a quiet family place it was when we were children," Angie reminisced.

"It's certainly not like that now," Helen commented. "Too big, too commercial, too crowded. I don't know that I'd bring a young family here."

"I would," Emily said, and suddenly Angie's eyes were shooting daggers at her. "Don't disagree with her" they were saying.

Oh dear, everything is going so well, Emily thought. Trying to smooth over rough feelings, she quickly added, "But I can see your point."

"Who would like some ice cream?" Angie asked. "I've got chocolate and peach from The Royal Treat."

"Peach for me," said Emily.

"Chocolate is my favorite," said Melinda.

"I'll help," said Helen. Everyone relaxed as Emily's gaffe was forgotten, and the conversation moved on to The Royal Treat having the best ice cream anyone had ever eaten.

"I'm so glad this week is almost over," Helen sighed. "I'm not doing this again. Now that Dad has passed, we won't have to."

After finishing her ice cream, Angie had gone back to the kitchen where they could hear her putting things away. Helen put her head in her hands as she sat at the table and sighed again.

Out of nowhere she said, "My mother was smart to die first."

"You haven't talked much about your mother," Emily said, seeing her opening. "I'd love to hear about her. What was her name."

"Julia. Dupré was her maiden name. She died several years ago of heart failure," Helen responded. "Heart trouble ran in her family. She outlasted her two brothers, but she never made it into her eighties. When our brother Frank died, I think it took something out of her. He had fought with our parents the night he died, and they parted in anger. I think that bothered her. It was an open wound.

"Here's Angie," she said as her sister joined them at the table. "I was just telling Emily and Melinda about Mom. I miss her so much."

Angie nodded and poured them all more lemonade then sat down at the table.

Helen continued, "She was the sweetest, nicest person. Let me show you an old picture I have of her," Helen got up to retrieve her purse from the sideboard. She drew out a black and white photo of her parents taken when they were in their thirties.

Mr. Skinnard looked much the same, only younger, with a smoother face and more hair at the temples. He had on a bathing suit, and the ocean was in the background. He had his arm around a petite blonde woman in a modest dark bathing suit characteristic of the forties. Mrs. Skinnard was standing as tall as she could, shoulders back, head held high, and still only reaching her husband's shoulder. She was smiling, appearing proud and happy to have her picture taken with the handsome man next to her.

"Helen, it occurred to me a while ago, and I didn't think to ask you about it until now, but we've never seen a wedding picture of our parents. We've seen photos of them dating, and then photos of them holding Arthur when he was born, but no wedding photos." Angie leaned over the picture.

"I think they couldn't afford it," Helen said. "They would have been married while the country was still in a depression. Maybe Mom couldn't afford a wedding dress, and she didn't want her picture taken to remind her of it."

"Sounds plausible," Angie said, but she didn't sound convinced.

"I love this photo," Helen said. "Our mother looks so happy. I tell myself that maybe she was happy, then, and it was only after year upon year of kowtowing to a difficult husband and five rammy children that she was worn down."

"What was she like?" Melinda asked. "She must have been very patient to put up with your father."

"Oh she was," Helen said. "But, sometimes—when he was angry and complained too much about her cooking or if he was screaming at one of us and turning purple with rage—she would just burst into tears and run upstairs to bed."

"Couldn't have been too pleasant for you children," Melinda commented.

"You sort of get used to it," Helen said. "You learn to withdraw a bit and go inside yourself. When it happens often, as it did with us, you learn to go numb, so it doesn't hurt you anymore. I used to sit there during their arguments and fantasize about who I would marry when I grew up. I would make sure that my husband was nothing like my father. He would be kind and gentle and never yell at his wife or children."

"And look how that worked out for you," Angie said with a sad shake of her head. "Lesley was so kind and gentle the whole world walked all over him."

"Well, I'm divorced now and doing better on my own," Helen said. "And I love my job as a bookkeeper for our high school, so I'm financially sound also."

"Getting back to your mother," Emily said, hoping she wasn't prying too much. "What do you remember best about her? Did she read to you at bedtime or play games with you in the afternoon? Did she give you words of advice that have helped you in your lives?"

Helen and Angie exchanged glances.

Angie said, "She was a reserved woman. She didn't talk much.

Mostly she cleaned and did laundry. I guess with five children, there wasn't much time for games and reading."

"Oh!" said Helen. "Now I do remember. There was one book she did read to me. It was *Lucky Mrs. Ticklefeather*, all about her house and her pet puffin Paul. Isn't that funny. It's the only time I remember her reading to me."

"No words of wisdom?" asked Emily. "My mother was constantly admonishing me to 'do this,' and 'don't do that.'" She chuckled at the memory.

"No," said Angie. "But she did take us shopping a lot. She cared about us looking nice. I don't think it was out of vanity. I think it was because she knew how cruel adolescent girls could be, and she wanted us to be ahead of the game when it came to our clothes."

"Sometimes," Melinda suggested quietly, "mothers offer advice that teenage girls don't even hear." She hoped Helen and Angie were not offended by this suggestion.

"So true," Helen said. "I doubt my daughter hears ninety percent of what I say to her."

"Do you remember the back stairs?" Angie interrupted and jokingly tapped Helen on the shoulders.

"When we were teenagers," she explained, "Our house had two sets of stairs, one going up from the front hall and one from the kitchen."

"Yes," Helen joined in, "And when we came home from clothes shopping with our Mom, she would instruct us to take our packages in the kitchen door and up the back stairs so our father wouldn't see them. I guess she was avoiding a confrontation over how much money she spent."

"And we were only too glad to do it," Angie added. "She often shielded us like that."

"One time I was scheduled for a spanking after dinner," Helen said. "It was that time I painted my name on the garage doors. Do you remember that, Ang?"

"No, I was too little, but Keith has told the story often enough."

Emily and Melinda didn't look at each other, careful not to acknowledge that they'd heard this story already.

"Well, Dad told me to go to my room and get ready to be spanked. As I went upstairs before him, Mom was coming out of the bathroom and she nodded her head toward the doorway like she was pointing out a place to hide. Somehow I understood her message and told our father I had to go to the bathroom. Then I went inside, locked the door, and refused to come out."

"I can't believe Mom did that!" Angie laughed. "Go against our father right to his face."

"Well, maybe I misunderstood her look and came up with the bathroom idea all by myself. I can't be sure now. But it worked. After a few hours, Dad relented and said he wouldn't spank me if I came out. And he was true to his word."

"Good for you," Angie said. "Did you ever get spanked again?"

"No. Although I might have been better behaved after that, knowing I wouldn't get away with that trick again."

"I would have loved to have met your mother," Emily said.

"We've made our mother sound rather meek, which she was." Helen was thoughtful. "And I think Ang and I tend to act that way around men also," she mused.

"But as Mom got older, she would occasionally stand up for herself and do something shocking," Angie recalled. "Do you remember that card game, Helen, and what Mom did?"

"Yes, what a card game! Angie and I were playing bridge with Mom and Dad, and Mom played a card that Dad didn't like. He wasn't actually angry; he was just annoyed and told her so. We were all drinking manhattans and suddenly Mom got up with her drink, went to Dad, and acted like she was going to pour it over his head." Helen paused and Emily pictured Mr. Skinnard's face in her mind.

"Luckily, Dad was in one of his good moods, and he laughed at her. She took that as encouragement, and she tipped her glass and poured just a few drops on the top of his head. We were so shocked! I prepared myself for an explosion of anger from Dad. But Mom just stood there with her drink in her hand; she probably couldn't believe she had just done that either, and Dad laughed again and said he deserved it. Then Mom went back to her seat and picked up her cards without a word. Angie and I were so sure we were about to witness a catastrophe, yet nothing else happened. We went back to playing cards, and no one said a word. I was so proud of Mom for sticking up for herself." Helen paused again.

"That's the difficult thing about our father; he was so unpredictable. If something went wrong, he might explode or he might laugh. You never knew. Sometimes he would play tricks on us and wait for us to giggle at his antics, but we were too afraid to.

Then he'd be angry that we hadn't played along with him. It was exhausting. That's why I love that story of Mom pouring her drink on Dad's head. She was taking a chance that it could have gone the other way. Luckily for all of us, it turned out alright."

"Maybe old age makes you braver and smarter," Angie reflected. "My husband and I have fewer fights now. We already know how it's going to end, so we just don't start."

"You're husband's a gem," Helen commented.

"Second time's the charm," Angie said, purposely misquoting the well-known adage. "I often wonder, though, what kind of life our Mom would have had if she hadn't married our Dad. She needed someone quiet and thoughtful, like herself, to appreciate her intellect and her talent."

"I think about that myself," Helen murmured. "Instead of screaming matches and infidelity, she might have had a comforting arm and gentle partner who brought her laughter instead of tears. Sometimes I hate Dad so much, but then you and I wouldn't be here."

"So you were punished a lot as a child?" Emily asked.

"You would think so from the way we talk about him, but actually, I don't recall much more than a swat on the bottom or being sent to my room," Angie said.

"Were the boys disciplined?" Emily probed.

"Their punishment was losing the car keys," Helen said. "I do have one memory, though, of seeing my father standing with his belt in hand and all three boys lying on their stomachs on a bed because he was going to whip them. He saw me in the hallway, and he closed the bedroom door. I must have been very young and the older boys in their early teens because, as they got older, they were never home long enough to be punished."

"Except to have the car keys taken away," Melinda reminded her. "Did you ever have them taken away from you? Either of you?"

"Not Helen, Miss Goody Two Shoes," Angie laughed, "but I did."

"As I recall," Helen interrupted. "They weren't exactly taken away. You threw the keys at them."

"What happened?" asked Emily.

"Well, I wanted to see a boy friend, not a *boyfriend*, as in a date, but just to hang out with my friend. I don't know what I was being punished for, probably coming in too late, which I often did, but the point is they forbade me to see him that night. I snatched up the car keys and said I was going anyway. They said I would be grounded for a month if I did.

"I went up to my bedroom and sulked for a while. Then I decided to go out anyway. As I was creeping down the stairs, my mother called out and asked me to come into their bedroom and talk to her. I did, and she could see I was dressed to go out when I should have been in my pajamas. Dad was awake, and he started yelling and threatening, and I just got so mad I took the car keys out of my purse and threw the keys at them on the bed. I said I didn't want to drive their stupid car anyway. Then I stormed downstairs, called my friend, and went outside to wait for him to pick me up."

"What happened when you eventually returned home?" Emily asked.

"I was grounded for a month, but it was worth it. You should have seen the look on their faces when I threw those keys at them. They were shocked that I could be so bold."

"What an exciting household you grew up in," Melinda said. "I'm almost jealous, even though my parents were very kind to me. I was an only child and always wanted a brother or sister for company."

"Speaking of brothers, we've met Arthur and Keith. Do you mind if I ask about your other brother?" said Emily.

Both sisters looked down at the table.

"We heard that he was killed in a motorcycle accident back in the eighties. You don't have to talk about him if you don't want to," Melinda said gently.

"That accident happened twenty years ago this week." Helen shook her head. "We were all married and living upstate by then. Our parents were staying here in Chalet House for a summer vacation, and Frank came to visit them. We don't know what was said between them, but when Frank became a teenager, he began to fight like crazy with our father. Frank was one of those people you might call a rebel. He questioned everything. It drove my father crazy."

"And he always championed the underdog." Angie smiled. "Although he wasn't perfect. I know he'd used drugs and had been divorced twice. But there was a pretty big age difference between him and me since I was the youngest. You knew him better than I did, Helen."

"Yes, I liked him the best of our brothers. He always treated me with respect and listened to my ideas. He never belittled me. He taught me how to play the guitar and introduced me to folk music. When he and his girlfriend were home from college on the weekends, we sat around and played guitars and sang songs by Joan Baez and Bob Dylan.

"We lost touch when he moved out West. The last conversation I had with him had to do with Mom. He was angry at Dad for the way he'd treated her over the years. I had forgotten about it until this afternoon."

Helen stopped talking for a moment and stared down at the melted ice cream in her bowl. They hadn't bothered to clear the table of dessert dishes yet. The messy sandwich crumbs and melting ice cream reminded her of her life.

"What do you remember of that conversation, Helen?" Emily didn't want to sound pushy, but Melinda was giving her an elbow in the ribs, indicating she thought it was important that the conversation keep going.

"He was telling me about the last night he had spent at home before he left for grad school. He had gotten up in the middle of the night to use the bathroom. As he opened his bedroom door, he saw Mom rush out of the master bedroom in tears—yelling behind her 'Richard, you're such an animal!'—and then flee downstairs. Of course, he had to pretend he didn't see that. But he never forgot."

They suddenly heard a rush of wind outside the house, interrupting their conversation. All four looked about them. The windows rattled in their frames, and the walls around them seemed to shift a bit, making them feel unbalanced. A draft sprang up from nowhere, ruffling their hair and cooling their cheeks, then quickly vanished.

The four women peered outside the windows, but the skies were blue, and the clouds were fluffy and unmoving. They looked at each in confusion. Then the wind stopped as suddenly as it had started.

Emily shrugged and resumed the conversation. "Your poor mother! Those were different times. Women took literally that marriage vow to obey their husbands." She stopped there. She didn't know what else to say.

"You never told me that story about Frank seeing Mom in the middle of the night," Angie said accusingly.

"Perhaps I wanted to forget it. It's funny how one memory will trigger another that's been buried for years. Anyway, it's all ancient history. Frank is gone, Mom is gone, and now Dad has joined her. I guess he'll have to be nicer to her in the afterlife."

"I think we should get going, Emily," Melinda said, sensing a need for the sisters to be alone now.

"Yes. We still have laundry to attend to before the guys get home, which will probably be any minute now. Thank you so much for having us over for lunch."

"Thank you for coming. And for the flowers," Angie said.

Helen and Angie accompanied Emily and Melinda to the door, sad to see them go. Their brothers would return, and the sisters would cater to them as their mother had so many years ago.

As they walked back to Suits Us, Emily asked Melinda, "Children or adults?"

"Still children."

They were no sooner back than they were interrupted by the telephone on the kitchen wall ringing.

"I didn't know anyone had this number," Emily said as she rose to answer it.

"Hello? Oh, Mary Jo!...No, we don't have any plans this evening. But the guys are out fishing, and I don't know how tired they'll be when they get home. They might just want to go to bed and sleep...Yes, I'll ask them and let you know. How did you get this number?...Oh, that's clever of you! What's your number again? I lost the grocery slip you gave me."

Emily scribbled a phone number on an envelope sitting on the counter. "And your address is 345 Pinecone Drive. Thank you. I'll call you back later." She hung up the receiver.

"Guess who that was? Mary Jo! She knows who this house belongs to and who the phone is registered to. Well, we have an invitation to cocktails this evening if the guys are up to it when they get home. I hope so. We can talk tomorrow about what we heard from Helen and Angie today."

They sat on the sofa, put their feet up, and enjoyed a few unscheduled minutes.

"How are things with you and Elvis?" Emily asked.

"We're okay now, but I'm worried about our future. When I'm in his house, I usually let him run the show, especially since he's self-employed. Most of the time I read and run errands for him if he needs anything. I've evolved into his girl Friday since I've lived there—almost a year now. But sometimes, I want to go somewhere on the spur of the moment or buy something that appeals to me without worrying about whether Elvis likes it. Usually, it's no problem. My independence doesn't threaten Elvis. Once or twice, I've just hopped in my car and gone back home to New Hampshire to check on things or visit my friends. But that picture of the Beatles caught him by surprise. He didn't like it and he said so. Which he has every right to, but, oh...I don't know. It happens, doesn't it, in relationships? What about you and Bob?"

"Bob and I haven't known each other as long as you and Elvis, and we're not living together, so I don't have your issues, but I remember them well. When I was married, my ex wanted everything decorated in dark colors like we were outfitting a cave, and I wanted everything open and filled with sunlight. It was a never-ending battle. I understand, though, that it's about more than décor. You and Elvis have never been married, so maybe this is the first time either of you has dealt with this issue. You're living in his house, but it's become your home too. Somehow he's got to understand that you need a space that's yours to feel cozy in. You can't always feel like a guest. In British novels, the lady of the house always has a sitting room. Does he have an extra bedroom you can use and set up in your own style?"

"I've thought of that, but I haven't asked him yet."

"Melinda! It's not like you to be shy."

"This relationship is so important to me. I don't want to jinx it, and I'm afraid I might have with that picture."

"I don't think so. He's not the sort of guy who would throw away a fabulous woman like you over a picture of the Beatles."

They sat in comfortable silence a while longer, Melinda feeling a little better after the consoling words of her friend. Emily, however, was not as confident as her friend was. Perhaps, being single for so long, Elvis could abandon a good relationship over something as flimsy as a painting that didn't fit with his home décor.

Moments later, they heard scuffling at the door and the men appeared, sunburned, smiling, and empty-handed.

"What? No fish?" Emily asked as they took off their damp jackets and shoes and left them in the kitchen.

"Only bluefish," sighed Bob. "And I refused to bring any back with me."

"It's the truth," said Elvis.

"Was it fun?" asked Melinda.

"Yes," replied Elvis. "I caught about thirty of those blues. And we had a fabulous lunch."

"You did?" Emily and Melinda said in unison.

"On the way back," Bob explained. "We did some not-so deep-sea fishing in an area where there were flounder, and we caught half a dozen. At the dock, they had a guy who filleted them right in front of us and cooked them up on a charcoal grill, so we had fresh flounder for lunch. It was delicious."

"I thought you didn't like fish," Emily said.

"I've never had fresh flounder like that. It's very mild and tender. It hardly tastes like fish. I could eat that again."

"So, it was a success?"

"Definitely," Bob said.

"Did Arthur and Keith talk about their father at all?"

"We didn't bring it up, but as we were heading back to shore, Arthur was pretty drunk and did say one strange thing."

"You didn't bring up Mr. S., but I did," Elvis reminded him. "I took advantage of Arthur's less than sober state and asked him why the police were calling his father's death suspicious. I told him that they'd been by to question us."

"Did he say why?" asked Emily.

"Not much, only that the reason they were stuck here had to do with some, and I quote Arthur, 'damned pajamas.' So I made the appropriate sound of surprise—because I was—and asked how pajamas could be a problem. He growled 'because we should have hidden them.' Then Keith said, 'Arthur, shut up.' And that was that. I couldn't get any more information."

"So he could have been strangled with a pair of pajamas!" Melinda said. "That's a new one."

"But whose pajamas were they?" Emily asked. "That's what we have to find out."

"But we haven't told you the best bit," Elvis added. "Mervin Crippens was waiting at the dock this morning to talk to Arthur and Keith."

"We couldn't hear everything he said," Bob told them. "But as he was leaving, he shouted out that Mr. and Mrs. Skinnard had never been married. He made a point of calling them all bastards."

"That's something," Emily said. "You need to tell me more about that."

"Not right now," Bob said. "I need a shower."

"After you clean up and rest a bit, would you guys be up for cocktails with an old friend of mine who lives a few blocks over?" Emily asked. "If the hors d'oeuvres are tasty, they could be our dinner."

"Shrimp cocktail?" Elvis asked.

"Crab dip?" Melinda suggested.

"We can always have pizza delivered when we get home if we don't get enough to eat," Bob said.

"Okay, I'll give her a call."

Emily phoned Mary Jo, and they agreed on a six o'clock date.

Bob said, "I'll have just enough time for a nap. Wake me at five-thirty."

CHAPTER TWELVE

COCKTAILS

Since the Smith residence was a mere four blocks away, the foursome decided to walk. The summer evening was warm and still, the best of late August weather, a time when you wish the season would never end. As they approached 345 Pinecone Drive, they found a tiny wooden arrow stuck in the dirt. The number 345 was painted in yellow, pointing down a narrow brick path under overhanging pines. The residence could not be seen from the road.

The four paused to look around them. Pinecone Drive was a hundred-year-old community of weathered stone mansions shaded by thousand-year-old pines drooping with dark needles like ancient brows over shuttered eyes. The spook factor was high, and the lack of streetlights on a cloudy night could send even the most intrepid of strangers scurrying back the way they came. On this peaceful evening, however, with the sun still lingering above the treetops, the four friends didn't hesitate to plunge into the shaded lane in search of their host.

Twenty steps later, they emerged into a lit courtyard and an astonishing burst of light gleaming from an old carriage house. The house had been refurbished with a second story of glass walls and steel beams, lit up from within by standing lamps and hanging lanterns.

"My word!" exclaimed Elvis, sounding like Sherlock Holmes upon discovering a clue.

"Indeed," said Bob as his Watson.

"I love it!" said Emily, and before Melinda could chime in, Mary Jo appeared at the entrance door on the ground floor and waved them in.

"So glad you found it," she called. "We're the rebels on Pinecone Drive. I couldn't stand to live in one of those dreary stone monstrosities."

On the ground level, two outlines where the carriage doors had once been were now covered over and painted in dark wood stains. The door to the upstairs was to the left of these, and they followed Mary Jo up to an open concept great room where two walls were glass. The third wall was kitchen cabinets, and the fourth wall was a fireplace behind which, Mary Jo explained, were two bedrooms.

"Perfect for empty nesters like Dan and myself," she said as a very bald and painfully thin gentleman joined them from a bedroom. "My husband," she said, introducing him. "And this is my friend Emily. Remember I told you I dated her brother in high school?"

Dan nodded. "Very pleased to meet you," he said.

Emily took over the introductions. "This is my friend Melinda, and our friends Bob and Elvis. It's very kind of you to invite us over this evening."

"We're glad for the company," Mary Jo replied. "We don't get much news from the outside or see folks from up North. Come have a seat in our living room and enjoy the view. We tried to angle the windows so we could get views of the sunrise and the sunset. What can I get you to drink? I can fix a martini or a manhattan. We have white or red wine and beer. What's your pleasure?"

Dan moved to the kitchen area and said, "I'll get them, dear."

"Just a beer for me," Elvis said.

"Me too," Bob echoed him.

"I'm fixing myself a manhattan," Dan said.

"Well, in that case," Bob reconsidered, "I'll have one too."

"Make that three," Elvis said.

"Great, I'll mix up a pitcher."

"White wine for me," Emily spoke up.

"Is chardonnay okay?" asked Mary Jo.

"Yes."

"Chardonnay for me also," said Melinda.

Drinks settled, everyone found a seat on a large circular sofa with deep cushions of sea mist green. The four guests began to relax. In the middle was a coffee table laden with snacks anyone might enjoy: barbequed shrimp wrapped in bacon, a creamy dip exploding with crab morsels, three choices of cheese, four choices of crackers, and little tacos that needed a bite to discover what was inside. No one would be leaving hungry.

"How are you doing, Emily?" Mary Jo asked. "Are you working?"

"I'm a loan administrator at Mirety Bank. Bob works there also," she added with a nod to him. "He's in Human Resources."

"And, you, Melinda?" Mary Jo asked.

"I'm a lady of leisure, I'm afraid. Although I help Elvis out sometimes in his business."

"How fortunate you are!"

"Well, yes, I am. But let's not talk about it." Melinda often felt useless and unimportant when the conversation turned to careers.

"Okay. And, Elvis, what do you do?"

"I'm self-employed. I write technical manuals for IT companies."

"I'm sure I don't even know what questions to ask about that. I can barely navigate my email. And you all seem to be single, right?"

The four responded with a chorus of yesses.

"Weren't you married, Emily? I thought I saw your wedding in the paper years ago."

"Yes. Unfortunately, it didn't work out. Luckily, there were no children."

"Sometimes they can be a solace. Dan and I were both married before. We have three children between us and five grandchildren."

Dan delivered the drinks, and the conversation lulled while everyone sipped their beverage and nibbled on the food laid out before them. The sun began to slide lower in the sky and paint the edges of clouds with apricot and lavender. Everyone admired the view.

"You know we're staying in the Suits Us cottage on Oak Avenue," Emily said to Mary Jo. "Melinda and I are always interested in the family histories of places where we stay. Are you aware of any tragedies that took place there?"

Melinda smiled at Emily's backdoor way of asking about the ghost she had seen.

"Why, no, not that I'm aware of," Mary Jo said. "The cottage has been a rental unit for years and years. I'd like to think I'm up enough on local gossip to have heard."

"I was just wondering," Emily replied.

Searching for a new topic of conversation, Emily noticed two sleek, polished rifles mounted over the fireplace. "Those rifles look like antiques," she said to Dan, nodding at the display. "Are you a collector?"

"Not really. Those guns belonged to my grandfather. I don't believe they work anymore. They're just for display."

"Do you have any other firearms?" Bob asked. "Mary Jo told Emily you used to be a detective."

"Just a few pistols for personal safety," Dan replied. "I keep them locked up, of course." He didn't offer any further information.

None of the four guests had any experience with guns or rifles and could think of nothing else to add. Mary Jo broke the uncomfortable silence.

"So, you just happened to rent a place next door to the Skinnards? How are they?"

"The father seemed very frail when we met him," Emily began. "He died Monday night."

"No! What a shame. I didn't see it in the papers."

"I believe they'll be sending his body to Dover, and the final arrangements will be handled there."

"So the kids have packed up and left?"

"No." Emily stopped. She wasn't sure what to tell them about the suspicious nature of the death and their being questioned by the police.

"They're worried about the storm predicted for this weekend causing damage to the house," Melinda spoke up. "They're going to stay until it's over."

"You know, I've seen them in the past, at a distance. I don't think they come every summer, but every few years or so, especially since their mother died. I've always admired their devotion to the old man."

"We went out to dinner with them Monday night. He seemed hard to please. They were all very tense around him," Melinda said.

"Well, they're done with that," Dan said.

"I couldn't figure out why they bothered," Elvis said. "Lots of kids just ignore their parents when they get old. Not that it's the right thing to do, but because their parents become so unpleasant to be around, like Mr. Skinnard."

"You see, that's it." Mary Jo looked at Dan and Elvis. "They do it because it's the right thing to do. I've been told that about Keith from women friends of mine. He'll do something just because it's the right thing to do, even if he hates doing it."

"What else can you tell us about the Skinnards?" Emily asked. "They're an interesting family. Is the beauty salon business the only business they've ever owned?"

"Well, they tried to make money in real estate, but it never panned out. At least, that's what my father told me. This happened years ago and involved Mr. Skinnard's father. They owned a lot of land in a little town southwest of Dover called Warren. After World War I, old Reginald Skinnard thought the government was going to build low-cost homes in the Dover area for the returning servicemen. He bought some land cheap and thought he would sell it back to the government at a profit. Well, it turned out the government bought land in Wilmington instead and built housing there on Union Street, so he was stuck with this land and no buyer."

"What did he do?" asked Emily

"He was a religious man and went to Sunday and daily mass at the local Catholic church, St. Sulpice. The nuns at the school there were from Ireland and were very poor, and the local farmers were even poorer. Neither had money to buy land for a parish school, although they badly wanted one. When Mr. Reginald died, he left that land to the church so they could build a school."

"How kind of him! Too bad none of that kindness was passed on to his son, Richard." Emily said.

Dan interrupted at this point. "You really shouldn't think too badly of old Richard. You met him at a low point in his life. Lots of us get crotchety as we age." He stopped to wink at Mary Jo. "Wait until you get a little older and wake up every morning with a backache, and your doctor tells you not to eat your favorite foods and to stop drinking alcohol as well. The list goes on and on. You'll be cranky too."

"I see your point," Bob said.

"Did you know one of Mr. Skinnard's friends named Mervin Crippens?" Emily asked.

Dan frowned and stood up abruptly. Without explanation, he walked over to the kitchen area. The others heard him banging cabinet doors so hard that the plates inside rattled.

Emily looked in alarm at Mary Jo. "Did I say something wrong?" she asked.

Mary Jo had lost her smile also. She said softly, "We don't mention that name in this house. Merv Crippens molested Dan's brother on a Boy Scout camping weekend."

"Did his parents report him to the police? Was he arrested?"

"You didn't talk about things like that in those days. They were too ashamed. Dan's brother was devastated. It would have been too painful to make him tell the police. And then the newspapers would get wind of it and his whole family would be shamed. They wouldn't have been able to go anywhere without people pointing at them and talking about them behind their backs. So no, they didn't tell the police."

"But he needed to be stopped," Bob said gently.

"Dan's parents told Richard Skinnard, and he saw to it that Merv lost his position with the Scouts," Mary Jo responded. "And Richard asked Dan's parents *not* to go to the police. He said he would handle it."

"I'm so sorry. What an awful thing for Dan's family to go through," Emily acknowledged.

"You forgot something, Mary Jo," Dan said angrily as he returned from the kitchen, fresh drink in hand.

"Richard never let Mervin forget about that incident. If Mervin wanted a promotion at his job, Richard would threaten to tell his boss about his proclivities. When his wife wanted to join Julia's bridge club, Richard threatened to tell all the women in the club. He made Mervin's life hell for about twenty years until Mervin finally moved away. I think he went down to North Carolina."

"We saw him recently," Emily admitted. "On the Rehoboth boardwalk and at Irish Airs in Lewis."

"Well, I better not see him," Dan said. "I might not be able to control my temper." He sat heavily on the sofa. Sweat was forming across his brow. "Mervin Crippens should have gone to jail."

"I wonder why Richard advised Dan's parents not to go to the police," Mary Jo said.

"Richard sponsored Mervin's application to the Boy Scouts to be a leader," Dan replied. "I hold him almost as responsible as Mervin Crippens. Richard gave Mervin access to all those innocent young boys. Richard had to have known."

"Maybe Richard also felt the shame attached to it," Mary Jo said, sighing.

Agitated even more, Dan got up and returned to the kitchen area with his empty glass.

"Where is your brother-in-law now?" Bob asked Mary Jo.

"He lives in Pittsburgh, but he's here in Rehoboth this week, staying at a campsite over near Angola. We've seen a lot of him and his partner this week. But let's not talk about that. Dan doesn't care for his brother's choice of company."

"What do you know about Mrs. Skinnard?" Emily asked.

"Unfortunately, almost nothing. She was very quiet. I know she played the piano, but only when she thought no one could hear her. When I was a teenager, I happened to walk by their house on a weekday in the early afternoon, and I heard the most beautiful piano music coming from inside. I knew it wasn't a recording. I thought some visiting musician must be staying there. I went up to the living room window and looked in between the blinds. Mrs. S. was at the piano, swaying back and forth, playing something dark and intricate. I was astounded by her virtuosity. You would almost call it passionate. I ran into Keith at a cocktail party once, and I used the opportunity to ask him about her. He said that if I ever met her, I should never mention it because she would stop playing. He was in awe of her."

Mary Jo shook her head sadly. "I also heard that she only had one or two friends. She hated to drive and seldom left the house. All she did was clean, do laundry, and play the piano."

"The poor woman," sighed Emily. "She sounds intriguing. I suppose Frank's death affected her deeply as well."

"I've heard so much about him from family and friends who know the Skinnards, but Frank is and always will be a mystery to me. He was very smart in school but just had to argue with everybody. I met him once at a dance, and he was fun to talk to. He would point out a certain person and try to create a funny personality out of what they were wearing or how they were standing."

"You said he died in a motorcycle accident out on Pilottown Road."

"Yes. Frank was visiting his parents one summer when they were staying in Chalet House—that was the only house they ever rented. There was an argument. Frank ran out. At least, that's what I heard. He left to go visit some friends at the University of Delaware facility out on Pilottown Road, but there was a terrible storm that night and the roads were treacherous. Not a good night to be riding a motorcycle. No one heard or saw a thing, but a fisherman found him floating in the canal the next morning. Come to think of it, this week is the twentieth anniversary of his death."

Dan returned with drink refills for everyone. He smiled as he passed them around, seemingly recovered and in a better mood now.

"Was he married? Did he have children?" Emily asked.

"I don't think he was married at the time, and as far as I know, he had no children," Mary Jo replied.

"How sad for the Skinnards," Bob said.

"You never want to lose a child, no matter how old they are," Dan commented.

"We've learned so much about the Skinnards in just these few days," Emily commented. "We know Arthur was upset at having to leave his private college when it was time for Frank to attend college also. And we've heard about Helen and her unhappy first marriage, and Angie's fear of monsters under her bed, but we haven't learned much about Keith."

"He's always kept a low profile," Mary Jo said. "But I can tell you one story about when his cover was blown. Are you interested?"

"Of course," smiled Elvis. "We're all amateur detectives here, and we haven't quite figured out what's going on over there. Please, tell us about Keith."

"Has he talked about his love of antique cars?" she asked.

"No," said Emily. "Nothing at all."

"Well, he has always loved to work on cars, and I probably wouldn't have known that myself except for this incident. You see, back when he was sixteen, he bought a beat-up old truck and hid it from his father."

"How do you hide a truck?" Bob asked. "You can't exactly sneak it into the basement."

"The Skinnards were living in a working-class section of Dover at that time, across from a block of rowhomes. In the middle of the block were garages, imagine a warehouse-sized building but all garage bays. The people in the rowhomes could rent them to park their cars in, only very few people actually did. Most of the garages sat empty and didn't even have locks on the doors. Keith parked the truck in one of the abandoned garages and didn't tell his father about it. He and his friends would spend all their spare time working on that truck, trying to turn it into a hot rod.

"Well, one of the rowhomes that bordered on the alley around the garages was owned by a writer for the *Dover Star*, a local newspaper. Every Saturday morning, he would be woken up by banging noises and Keith and his friends talking as they worked on that truck. He wasn't angry about the noise, but he was curious about the banging. One Saturday morning, he decided to go down to the garages and discover what's going on. He found Keith and his friends and was pleasantly surprised at their initiative and hard work. In fact, he took a picture of them, and went home and wrote an article for the newspaper. Can you imagine Mr. S. sitting at his kitchen table having his morning coffee, and opening the paper to see his son involved in something he knows nothing about?"

"We saw what a control freak he was," Emily said. "I can imagine his anger."

"All of Dover saw that story. I remember my father pointing it out to my mother over his morning coffee."

"Do you know if Keith was punished?" Melinda asked.

"I did learn what happened, but it wasn't as bad as you're thinking. I saw Keith at a Christmas party when we were all home from college one year, and I asked him about it. He laughed and said his father accused him of being possessed when it came to that truck, and that it wasn't healthy. Mr. S. said if he wanted a car so bad, he would buy him one, but Keith had to get rid of that old truck." Mary Jo paused to sip her wine.

"Did he?" Melinda asked.

"Yes, Keith did, and his father bought him a used car that ran."

"That's one of the kinder family stories that we've heard," Emily said. "What an interesting group. We've only known them a few days, and I feel like I know them better than my own family."

With nothing more to say about the Skinnards, they moved on to talk about the design of the carriage house and, then, books and movies of mutual interest.

After he caught himself falling asleep during a discussion of the upcoming football season, Bob suggested it was time to leave. "We've been up since very early this morning, and I'm afraid three manhattans have finally caught up with me," he apologized. "Thank you so much for having us over for cocktails and these scrumptious shrimp and crab dishes."

"You are very welcome," Mary Jo said as they all rose to leave.

"Please come back. Maybe you'll come to Rehoboth again next year?"

"I think that's a great idea," Emily said.

"I second that," Elvis said. "Thank you so much."

Mary Jo followed them down the stairs and out into the night. "One more quick story about Richard Skinnard," she said. She turned her back to the closed door while she spoke to them.

"You know that before we moved to Wilmington and my mom opened a hair salon in our basement, we used to live in Dover. It was before I was born, so I guess my mother was quite young. Anyway, my mother worked in the Skinnard beauty salon for a month or so until she was fired for not wearing a girdle."

"Really?" Melinda gasped. "She could be fired for that?"

"Mr. S. insisted all his hairdressers wear skirts, nylons and girdles. He said he could tell just by looking at a woman's derriere if she had on a girdle or not. My mother didn't feel like wearing a girdle one day and thought he wouldn't notice. He did, and he didn't even give her a warning. He just told her she was fired and to leave at once."

"No Human Resources department at the Skinnard salons," Bob joked.

"Don't laugh," Mary Jo said. "My parents were poor. It was just after the war, and my father was out of work at the time. Mom losing her job created a real hardship for my parents. She never forgave Mr. S. My dad was a bit of a rough fellow; he threatened to kill him. But, of course, he didn't. We were never allowed to mention his name."

"No tears for the departed Mr. Skinnard in your home," Elvis commented.

"No, no tears here. Take care walking home." Mary Jo opened the door so they could leave.

"Thanks again," the four echoed as they left.

Elvis had brought a flashlight, which helped them find their way out to Pinecone Drive. The lights from the other houses illuminated the road, and they soon returned home.

"That was a great evening," Bob remarked when they arrived back at Suits Us. "But I'm going immediately to bed before I fall over."

"And I am going to join him. Good night, all," Emily said.

"Good night," said Melinda and Elvis together.

"What did you think about all the new information we have about the Skinnards?" Emily asked Bob as they lay in bed.

"Interesting, but not much help if you're trying to solve a murder."

"I see your point," Emily said. "But what about the story about Frank and the fight with his parents? Perhaps the siblings blame Mr. S. for Frank's death," she suggested.

"I think they would have exacted their revenge by now."

"Or maybe that Mervin guy snuck into the house and killed him."

"Really, with four other adults there?"

"We don't know anything about how the family fortune is to be distributed," Emily continued. "Maybe one or two of the siblings wanted to murder their father because they need the money."

"Now that's an idea," Bob yawned.

"They're here, in Rehoboth, not at home where law enforcement knows who they are. It might be easier to get away with murder in a busy beach town."

"I see that," Bob agreed. "But I still think you're off base. The autopsy will probably find that the father died of natural causes."

"Let's just hope no one else dies while we're here," Emily said.

With that sobering thought, they both fell asleep.

FRIDAY

CHAPTER THIRTEEN

THE EYES

Friday morning, the four decided to go shopping at the Tanger outlets on Route 1.

"Like I don't have enough clothes?" Emily sighed as she finished the French toast Elvis had prepared for breakfast—French toast that melted in her mouth and coaxed her to go on eating even after she was full.

"But still, I love to shop, and after a week of Elvis's cooking, I probably need to replace my entire wardrobe in the next larger size."

"You can always shop for Christmas presents," Bob suggested with a wink. "My work shirts get worn out quickly from the harsh detergents and starches they use at the cleaners. I'll give you my neck and arm measurements before we leave."

"Great idea! Please do that."

"And I'll need your sizes, also, so I can shop for you."

"Just buy everything in large. No, wait, I should be back to a medium by the holidays."

"And you, Melinda?" Elvis called from the kitchen. "What shall I get for you?"

"Oh, don't even try to shop for me; I like crazy things—shawls and scarves and wild colors. Gift certificates work best. Or we can go shopping together and I'll tell you what to buy me. Then, by Christmas, I will have forgotten what you bought."

They were at the shops by ten and exhausted from shopping by noon. Emily's weakness was shoes, and while she'd found three shirts for Bob, she'd also found two pairs of sandals on sale and some low boots to wear with jeans in the fall.

They met back at the car; all four weighed down with shopping bags. Melinda had a bag of jellybeans she passed around.

"Can't go too long without a treat," she said. "Please, help yourselves."

They drove across the highway to Sam's Seafood House. As they exited Bob's MDX, they couldn't help but notice dark clouds on the horizon.

"That's Hurricane Edgar," Bob said. "you guys haven't been paying attention to the news, but I have. This is going to be a strong storm. Let's have lunch then head back."

The restaurant was packed, but the hostess found them a table in the back. The air conditioning was ramped up to what must have been a bone-chilling sixty-five degrees, and the women went back to the SUV for sweaters.

"Why do they waste electricity like this?" Emily complained. "I just don't understand why restaurants do this."

"Maybe it's to keep the wait staff comfortable," Elvis suggested.

"I hadn't thought of that, but they should be thinking of their customers. I doubt I'll want to come back here."

"We're leaving tomorrow anyway, probably like most onetime customers," Bob pointed out. "But, I agree with Elvis, it's the wait staff's argument."

All four ordered burgers and Guinness.

"Beer for lunch, girls?" chided Bob.

"Last day of vacation," said Melinda.

"But you're always on vacation, trust fund baby," Elvis chuckled.

"She's joining me in my mourning," Emily said.

Lunch was delicious and filling, and they were back to Suits Us by two o'clock to begin the sad chore of packing up.

The skies continued to darken, and rain threatened to fall.

Melinda glanced outside at Chalet House's garden and spied the child Helen sitting in one of the large lounge chairs, the lower half of her little body covered with a crocheted afghan blanket. She was looking self-absorbed, lost within herself, examining a world that no one else could see.

This was the first time Melinda had seen any of the siblings as a child outside of the house. She felt it meant that she should speak to her.

Without saying anything to the others, she went outside to join Helen.

"Are you okay, Helen? Is something bothering you?"

"I had the bad dream again last night," she said in a tiny voice.

"What bad dream? Can you tell me about it?"

Melinda sat down in the chair next to her.

"You won't believe me." Helen raised her right hand and caught a bunch of her blonde hair in her fingers and began to twist it round and round.

"Why wouldn't I believe you? A dream is not something you believe or don't believe. It is what it is. Something you experience in your sleep."

"Then you won't laugh at me?"

"Of course not."

"Okay. Well, in my dream, I've gotten a new pair of shoes, shiny black patent leather shoes, with one strap and a buckle on the side. They're called Mary Janes. Do you know what kind I'm talking about?"

"Of course. I had shoes like that when I was little."

"Well, I bring them home and put them in my clothes closet."

"Okay," Melinda responded, encouraging her to continue.

"Here's the hard part. In the morning, when I wake up, I go to the closet and open the door—you're not going to believe what happens next."

"I promise,"—Melinda smiled—"I'll believe you."

Helen let go of her hair and pulled the afghan closer against her chest.

"A golden eye comes out of each shoe and rises about level to my head and just floats in the air so that a pair of eyes is staring right at me. There's no head, no body, just eyes. They follow me everywhere, and they never go away. When I go downstairs to breakfast, or go to school, or just walk down the street, they are always behind me, following me, watching me. Then I wake up."

"Do other people see the eyes?"

"No, that's another scary part. No one else can see them but me. And the eyes never leave me alone."

Helen closed her eyes and tears began to trickle from her pale lashes. Melinda got up and went to sit on the edge of Helen's chair. She placed her arm around Helen's shoulders. Although she knew on one level that this was a spirit manifestation, she was surprised to find that there was corporeal flesh for her to pat and hug.

Helen lay her head on Melinda's lap and sobbed softly.

"You do believe me, don't you?" she said.

"Of course," Melinda crooned and smoothed Helen's hair with her free hand. She kissed the top of her head. She decided that this Helen was too young to discuss the meanings of dreams. Comfort was the most immediate need.

The child Helen was quickly soothed. From under her blanket she pulled a yellow piece of material and dabbed her eyes with it.

"What have you got there?" Melinda asked.

Helen held up the cloth, opening it out so that Melinda could see it was a pale-yellow pajama top with eyelet lace around the neck.

"Is that yours?" Melinda asked.

"No, it was my mother's. I saved it when she died."

Her tears stopped, and she pulled away from Melinda's embrace.

"That looks like the top half," Melinda said. "Where are the bottoms?"

"It's a secret," the child whispered.

"You can tell me," Melinda prompted. "I wouldn't tell anyone."

"Not today. Maybe tomorrow."

"You can talk to me any time," Melinda told her.

"I will," Helen said. Melinda glanced away for a moment at the dark skies threatening rain, and when she looked back, the adult Helen was now sitting next to her. She didn't seem at all surprised that Melinda was there and had her arm around her.

A chill breeze rushed over them and they both shivered. The pines sighed. The women looked up simultaneously as heavy drops began to pepper their bare arms.

"Time to go in," Helen said. "Thank you for listening."

Melinda watched Helen return to Chalet House and thought about the yellow pajama top. She'd have to tell Emily.

CHAPTER FOURTEEN

THE STORM

Back inside, the others greeted Melinda with the news that Hurricane Edgar had been upgraded to a Category 2 storm, was picking up speed, and should be making landfall in Rehoboth between 8 and 10 p.m. They searched the house for candles and matches, luckily finding plenty. Their search also yielded two filled oil lamps.

"Let's eat as much of our refrigerated food as possible for dinner tonight," Bob said. "We'll probably lose power, and the food will go bad."

"We haven't much left anyway," Emily replied. "It's the end of the week, and we're leaving tomorrow."

"If we're in the midst of a hurricane, roads could be closed or blocked by fallen trees," Elvis pointed out. "We might not be able to leave when we want to."

"We can worry about that tomorrow," Bob said. "Let's just get through tonight."

"We'll be fine," Melinda said, with an undertone of doubt betraying her confidence.

Elvis picked up on it. "Hurricane party!" he crowed. "Isn't that what they do in New Orleans, or Florida, or any of those places where hurricanes happen all the time?"

"We've got some mixers left and some lemons and limes. I'll be the bartender," Bob offered. "What kind of drink would you ladies like?"

"I've been dying for a vodka martini," Emily said. "And since this is a dire situation, I think I'll chance it. We're not out in public, so if I get drunk, folks, please be kind."

"One vodka martini with a twist of lime coming up. And you, Melinda? What's your pleasure?"

"Just a mild vodka and tonic. I have a feeling I'm going to need my wits about me tonight."

"No problem. And you, my Poe-loving friend? May I point out that the hurricane is named after your favorite writer? That can't be good."

"I'm with Melinda on this one. If this hurricane does any damage and we're wandering around in the dark, I don't want to be drunk. I'll just stick to Guinness."

"Coming up. Now, who is doing the honors as cook?"

"I believe it's my turn," Elvis volunteered and went to the refrigerator. The other three smiled and knew it wasn't his turn at all and that he preferred to cook so he could prepare meals to fit his taste.

"One pound of hamburger, one onion, one package of hamburger rolls, eight slices of cheese, and one bottle of ketchup. Seems obvious to me; burgers it is."

A chorus of groans went up.

"We had burgers for lunch," Bob mumbled.

"Then I shall be forced to fix them a little differently than you're used to—that is, Elvis style."

"Promise me you're not using bananas and peanut butter," Melinda said, referring to Elvis Presley's favorite sandwich.

"We don't seem to have those ingredients, or at least not enough peanut butter to go around," Elvis answered.

"Thank goodness. I don't think I could swallow a burger with a peanut butter and banana topping."

"Not to worry. Anything I concoct will be amazing. Is the grill available? Isn't it sheltered under an overhang?"

"Yes, but you'll still get wet because of the wind," Emily said.

"Wet, schmet. Who cares if I can impress you once again with my culinary skills? Now sit back and wait to enjoy the best burgers you've ever eaten."

And Emily, Bob, and Melinda did just that. They watched the dire predictions on TV showing where Hurricane Edgar would strike, and how soon, and enjoyed their beverage of choice. The good news was that the storm would be veering off to the northeast and Rehoboth would only get the edge of it. Edgar would be out to sea by early morning.

Thirty minutes later, Elvis appeared with a tray of burgers, served on toasted buns, decorated with lettuce leaves, tomato slices, and individual servings of potato chips in fancy finger bowls.

"Where's the ketchup?" asked Bob.

"In the burger," answered Elvis.

"It is!" exclaimed Melinda. "Along with the onion and the cheese. It's delicious! I've never had a burger like this. It's more like a mini meatloaf, and I love the toasted bun. Perfect, Elvis. Like everything you do." She got up and kissed him.

Only after everyone had finished their burgers and a plate of cookies had been passed around did Melinda remember her talk with Helen.

"Guys, I almost forgot to tell you. I was speaking to Helen this afternoon as she sat in the backyard. She was telling me about a bad dream, and she started to cry. Then she wiped away her tears with a piece of yellow clothing that turned out to be a pajama top. Elvis, didn't you say something about the police finding pajamas near Mr. Skinnard?"

"I did. Arthur said that's why the death is being investigated as suspicious."

"So what does Helen having a pajama top with her mean?"

"Well, I would think the police would have confiscated the pajamas found with Mr. S.," Bob said.

"Just a coincidence then?" Emily asked.

"That would be my guess," Elvis said.

"I don't like coincidences," Emily murmured as they felt the cottage shudder from a sudden, fierce blast of wind.

At Chalet House, they were halfway through dinner when they lost power.

"Looks like we hand wash the dishes tonight," Helen commented.

She got up to fetch candles.

"You might not have noticed," Keith said, "But this place still doesn't have a dishwasher."

"Oops, I forgot. Of course! It's a wonder you've noticed since you haven't washed a dish all week."

"That's women's work."

"Have you been living under a rock, Keith," Helen said as she placed two candles on the table and lit them. "There is no more 'women's work.' We all share equally."

"Not at my house. God, I'm sick of this place. I can't wait to get home. One more night. I want a shower with some decent water pressure and the loving arms of my wife. Along with her cooking." Keith said this with a sideways glance at Arthur.

"I'm in too good a mood to rise to the bait tonight," he replied. The sisters both knew that Arthur's wife was an excellent cook as well. It was one more rivalry between the two men as to whose wife could prepare the better meal.

The men moved to the living room area where more candles had been placed to lighten the gloom. They could hear the wind pick up outside and whistle through the pines. The rain began in earnest and beat down on the roof, reminding them of another hurricane they had survived in this very house. In 1954, Hurricane Carol had blown by offshore and luckily left little damage. Helen had been six years old, Angie three.

"Not much to do," Arthur said. "Keith, let's play cards while we wait for Helen and Angie to do the dishes."

Next door, the four were finishing dinner and tracking the storm on TV. They noticed that black clouds had darkened the sky so much it was as if night had fallen. The wind was now a constant howl. As it buffeted the pines, the gale created whooshing noises that worried even the men, though they didn't speak of it. The rain was a steady staccato on the roof, so loud they had to turn up the volume of the TV.

The pines moaned and swayed, and the rain pounded down. The four looked nervously at the ceiling, the walls, and each other.

"The pines rarely come down in a storm," Emily tried to reassure them. "They have very flexible trunks."

"But they do sometimes, right?" Melinda asked.

"Well, I guess so, but not too often," Emily replied.

The TV weather gurus were joined by local newscasters who explained that Route 1 between Dewey and Bethany Beach was closed, and all residents of Rehoboth, Dewey, and Lewes were urged to stay inside and off the roads until further notice. If someone needed to go to the hospital, they should call 911 rather than try to make the trip themselves.

The Baltimore meteorologist informed them that the winds were now up to seventy miles per hour, which made Edgar a Category 1 hurricane. They saw film clips of the waves crashing over the Rehoboth and Ocean City boardwalks; so far, no businesses had lost their storefronts. Footage of Route 1 along Towers Beach showed the highway completely underwater.

"Time for another round of drinks," said Bob.

"Here, here," said Elvis.

While Bob went to the kitchen, the three continued to watch TV, absorbed by the damage of the storm and the power Mother Nature was unleashing.

"On some level, I enjoy knowing that there is a power greater than human power. I don't know why," Elvis commented.

"Because you're nuts," Bob said and handed him another Guinness.

"I know what you mean," Melinda agreed. "It's like a child wanting to know that his parent is there to catch him if he falls. Unfortunately, Mother Nature can't do anything if we decide to blow ourselves up or poison ourselves out of existence."

"Here, you need a drink," Bob said, and handed her another vodka tonic. Then the lights went out.

"Oh no," Emily groaned. "Already? I was hoping this wouldn't happen until we were asleep."

"You expected to sleep tonight?" Melinda asked. "I don't think I can with all this wind howling outside."

A match flared and an oil lamp lit up.

"Here's some light," Bob said and placed the lamp on the coffee table. "Is that better?"

"Thank you!" Pleased, Emily stood up to kiss him.

In the semidarkness, they sat and tried to talk of other things without betraying how worried each was. They discussed their plans for when they returned to Wilmington, what chores would be facing them, what amenities they would be glad to return to, what email awaited on their computers, and how they missed their usual routine.

They talked and talked through the gloom until they finally sat in silence. Suddenly, they heard a knock at the door. Everyone jumped.

"Who could that be?" Emily asked.

Elvis was at the door in two seconds and opened it to find Keith standing under an umbrella in the pouring rain.

"Come in," he said. "Is everything alright?"

"I'm too wet to come in," he said. "I see you've lost power too. We figured this would happen, what with the hurricane and all. We are totally bored with no TV, and the candlelight isn't good enough to read. Why don't you four come over and we'll play some games or something until we're tired enough to sleep. Honestly, when we four get together and we don't have anything to do, we usually end up fighting. You'll be doing us a favor to come over and help us kill some time."

The four looked at each other and shrugged their shoulders. "Why not?" their expressions said.

"Can we bring anything?" Emily asked.

"Do you have any wine? We've drunk most of ours."

"I think we have a few bottles," Elvis said.

"Great," Keith replied. "I'll go back and tell the others that you're coming." Keith disappeared back into the rain and wind.

"This feels weird," Elvis said. "Any prickling of your thumbs, Melinda?"

"I'm afraid so. I'd say treat them gently, like the oversized children they are. And hope no trees fall on either house tonight."

The four arrived at the front door of Chalet House promptly at 8 p.m. with three bottles of wine and two dripping umbrellas. Before they could knock, the door was opened by Keith, with damp tousled hair and a grin that said "Ready to party."

However, "Thanks for the wine" is what he said to them as he took the bottles from Elvis and motioned them to sit down at the table, where Arthur, Helen, and Angie were waiting for them. In between the candles were more bottles of wine already opened, half-filled glasses, bowls of chips and dip, and a shiny top hat sitting upside down on the table.

Emily, Bob, and Elvis saw four adults worried by the storm but glad to ease that concern with the company of their neighbors. Melinda saw a teenage Keith and Helen, a mature twenty or so Arthur, and a ten- or eleven-year-old Angie. She was glad to see the kids were happy for company.

Late August was always a dangerous time in Rehoboth Beach. And each Skinnard sharply remembered the momentous year of 1954 when three hurricanes had lashed the Delaware shore beginning with Carol on August 31, to be followed by Edna on September 11, and then Hazel on October 15. Hazel had left one dead behind her.

Arthur sat at the head of the table and announced they were going to play one of their favorite games from childhood, Truth or Dare.

"Uh-oh" mouthed Emily to Bob.

"Can't wait," spoke up Bob. "There's lots I don't know about

Emily. I hope I'm about to find some things out!"

"How will you know I'm telling the truth?" Emily asked.

"You're a terrible liar," he told her. "But I'm not going to tell you how I know. I need to keep that for future reference."

"We'll see if there is a future," she joked and poured him a generous serving of merlot. "Let me get you drunk and, then, your secrets will come out."

After stowing the new bottles of wine in the fridge, Keith joined them at the table.

"Okay," Arthur began, "Do you all know how to play Truth or Dare?"

"I've played a couple different versions," Elvis said. "How do you get started?"

"We choose a name from a hat, and that person gets to pick on someone to ask a question for Truth or Dare. Then that person chooses the next person for Truth or Dare," Keith explained. "Since you're our guest, how about if you, Elvis, put your hand in the hat and pick out a name. Oh, one more thing first. We always have a prearranged penalty for someone who refuses to either answer the question or accept the dare. Angie, do you want to tell everyone what that is? You were the last one to get this penalty—what was it—five years ago?"

The other siblings laughed, and Angie blushed. "The penalty is that you have to run around the block naked."

"You have to streak?" Emily cried. "Here in Rehoboth?"

"As I recall from recent walks," Elvis observed, "this is a huge block, about a quarter of a mile around."

"I wish I had known," Bob said. "I'd have hidden a towel in the bushes."

"It would have gotten soaking wet," Emily observed.

"A wet towel is better than no towel," Bob replied.

"Why didn't I think of that?" Angie lamented. "It always seems to be me that gets stuck with the penalty."

"Only because you're the one who doesn't want to reveal all the stupid things you've done in your life," Arthur chided her.

"Because you're so frigging judgmental," she shot back.

"Children, children, we have guests," Keith reminded them. "Ready, Elvis?"

Elvis put his hand in the top hat and pulled out a piece of folded paper. He unfolded it and read "Melinda."

"Okay, Melinda," Arthur instructed her. "Now you choose any person at the table and ask them a question—something personal—the juicier, the better. They have to answer, and if they won't, then you get to dare them to do something."

"Like what?" Melinda asked.

"Eat something disgusting like a spoonful of mustard, or do something ridiculous like lick the floor."

"Okay." She turned to Keith. "Have you ever had to run naked around the block?"

"That's too easy. No, I've never had to run naked around the block. My life is an open book. Now I get to ask a question. I have an easy question for you, Melinda. You have an odd accent. Where are you from?"

"I'm from New Hampshire, so it's not a down-easter accent, and we don't drop our 'r's' like the folks from Massachusetts, but my speech does have a New England ring to it."

"Okay," said Keith. "Now pick someone else to ask Truth or Dare and, everyone, make your questions a little harder. That's where the fun is."

Melinda turned to her friend. "Emily, I hope this doesn't embarrass you too much, but how old were you when you first had sex."

Emily paused for a moment. Did Melinda already know the answer? She wasn't sure if they had discussed this or not. She recognized the question was just personal enough to show that they were committed to the spirit of the game without delving into anything too horribly confidential.

She slowly sipped her wine for suspense, then answered, "Eighteen." She hoped Bob had been at least that old himself, and if not, she hoped it wouldn't matter. It was a topic that hadn't come up between them so far, thus the danger of the game.

"Now it's your turn, Emily," Arthur said. "Pick someone and ask a question."

"Arthur, what is the most scared you've ever been in your life?"

"I don't even have to think about that. It was the cherry bomb incident. Do you remember that one, Keith?"

"Do I ever. But you tell the story. I think our guests will enjoy it."

"One Sunday morning," Arthur began, "We were supposed to get up at seven o'clock to get ready for church. At that time, we three boys all slept in the same room. All of us had been out late the night before. Frank and I were home from college that weekend, so

I guess Keith was about fifteen."

"I may have been only fifteen," Keith interrupted, "but I had snuck a few beers the night before, so I was a little hungover myself."

"Well," Arthur continued, "It seems that Mom couldn't wake us up. She'd shake us, and we'd murmur that we'd get up, and then go right back to sleep. After ten minutes or so, Dad wasn't having any more of it. He came upstairs with a cherry bomb and an empty metal wastebasket. He stood in the center in the room, lit the cherry bomb, and dropped it in the wastebasket. Then he ran out. Boom! I think we were lifted a foot off our beds. I thought the Russians had dropped an atom bomb." Arthur laughed and smacked the table.

"After the cherry bomb exploded, Dad came back in the room and repeated his command for us to get up and get dressed. Believe me, we did, and we were quick about it. My ears were ringing all day."

"Holy cannoli!" Elvis laughed. "Your dad was some jokester."

"It wasn't a very nice joke. I don't think I ever forgave him for it."

"On to the next question," Keith said. "Arthur, your turn."

"Helen," he began, looking directly at his younger sister, who had been very quiet up to that point. Her hair was unwashed and uncombed; it fell in lank silver strands around her pale face. Her eyes were heavy from lack of sleep. But she smiled at him when he said her name.

"My question has two parts. Why *did* you marry that wimpy man that no one liked, and then why did he divorce you?"

"Didn't you ask me this once before?" she said, shrugging. "Well, maybe I just feel like you did. Anyway, my husband was nonjudgmental—unlike my family, as you may have observed," she added, nodding to the guests. "I felt relaxed around him. He wasn't scrutinizing my every gesture, my every move, my every decision. He made me feel loved for who I was."

No one commented on her appraisal of her siblings.

"And the divorce?" Arthur probed. "I know the new wife is fifteen years younger and has bigger tits. Was that it?"

Oh my, thought Emily, *he's embarrassing her. I hope we can end this game soon.*

"I don't think so. She is a musician. Lesley wanted to be a musician. They shared a common interest. It was that simple."

"So, it wasn't sex. I mean, sooner or later, doesn't it all come down to sex?" Angie asked.

"You can't ask me a question," Helen replied. "It's not your turn. It's mine. And I'm going to ask you, since you brought up the subject, Angie, to your knowledge, has your husband ever cheated on you?"

Angie swallowed and suddenly fought back tears.

The guests all began to feel uncomfortable. They hadn't planned on an evening of siblings airing each other's most intimate secrets or grievances. It was a simple yes or no answer. And how would they know if she was lying?

Angie looked at Helen and said, "No. My turn."

"Arthur, when I was growing up, I have no memory of you at all. Where were you? Why don't I remember you?"

"As you recall, baby sis, I'm twelve years older than you. When I came home from school, I was given the baby buggy and shown the door and told not to come back until dinnertime. The moment you were old enough to be left in a playpen with a few toys, I took off. I was tired of being the babysitter. You didn't see me because I was never there. It was not a happy household, and I didn't want any part of it."

Angie, not smiling, looked down at the table.

"Now I think we've neglected out guests with our family squabbling. It's my turn." Arthur smiled at the newcomers.

"Elvis, how did you get your name? Was your mom a fan?"

"She was, and she had all his records."

"Now it's your turn to ask someone a question," Arthur said.

Elvis turned to Melinda. "Have you always had this gift of seeing people's auras and having visions?"

The siblings were surprised to hear this about their guest. She hadn't done or said anything to indicate she had unique talents.

"As long as I can remember," she replied. "Only when I was little, I thought everybody could see what I was seeing. When I was around four, I started pointing out to people that I could see colors all around them, and my parents thought my eyes were bad. They took me to an ophthalmologist who explained that my eyes were fine and that he'd had other patients who spoke of seeing auras and feeling an empathy for people. He told my parents it was a special gift, but they'd have to teach me to keep what I was seeing to myself."

"I wish I could do that," Angie sighed. "I'm so bad at reading people."

"Sometimes it can be a curse," Melinda said, "when you know someone is lying and you can't prove it any other way. Then there are times when it doesn't seem to work at all. I haven't seen auras at all this past week," she hedged. She wasn't going to share with the Skinnards how she had seen them instead.

"Well, I'm glad I don't have anything like that," Helen said. "I have a hard enough time trusting people as it is."

Melinda turned to Elvis. Her green eyes had a twinkle.

"Elvis, I never got around to asking you why you have so many references to Edgar Allan Poe in your house."

"That's easy," he said. "I'm a direct descendant on my mother's side."

"I didn't think Edgar Allan Poe had any children," Bob said, puzzled.

"Well, not that you'll read about in Wikipedia. But my family claims he had an affair before his marriage that resulted in a line that comes down to me."

"Interesting. Well, because you're a guest, we'll give you the benefit of the doubt," Arthur said. "Unless you want to challenge him, Melinda?"

"Oh no. I trust Elvis," she smiled. Like his hair, his aura was white, a sign of purity. "Now you get to ask a question," she said to him.

Elvis turned to Bob. "You have been so quiet this evening, my man. In fact, you are always quiet. What are you hiding? Tell me something we don't know about you that might surprise us."

Bob sat up as if woken from a daydream. He had been thinking of what they would do tomorrow. He didn't want to leave Rehoboth just yet. If they could stay another few days, he was hoping to do more sightseeing or drive out to Trap Pond and look for the cypress swamp.

"Uh, something you don't know about me?" he stalled.

"Come on, Bob," Melinda teased him. "You really don't share much about what you do when you're not at work or hanging out with us."

"I think he reads a lot," Emily offered, trying to cover for him. She guessed that he spent most of his time watching TV and napping.

"Well, if you insist, I will tell you my dirty secret," Bob said.

"That's the spirit!" Keith was excited. "You watch porn, don't you?" he shouted. "We all do that, don't we, Arthur? I won't tell your wife. It'll be our secret."

"I'm a happily married man," Arthur growled. "I don't need that crap."

"That crap is what keeps us happily married and out of the bars," Keith laughed.

"Shut it, boys," Angie said. "I'm waiting for Bob to answer the question. Tell us your dirty secret, Bob."

Angie leaned in and winked at him. "We promise we won't tell anyone else. I mean, who would we tell? We'll all go back to our separate boring lives tomorrow and never see each other again. So, what is it?"

No one else spoke, and suspense began to build. Emily and Melinda glanced at each other. They were all a little drunk by this point and tongues were loosened. What would he say? Emily was almost frightened. Would it be something so embarrassing she'd have to reconsider their relationship?

As they waited for Bob to answer, the tumult outside caught their attention. The wind seemed stronger, the shutters rattling constantly now. And layered in with the rattle was a moan. It was the wind, moaning like an old woman writhing in grief.

Melinda was worried for Emily. Who knew what Bob might say? Would she be up tonight consoling her friend?

They heard Bob draw in his breath and watched him look around the table, gauging the crowd for their reaction. Then he bowed his head and, with his hands around his bottle of beer, spoke to the table. Out came his shocking revelation: "I play the accordion."

At first, everyone was quiet. Had they heard him correctly? He played the accordion. Then, all at once, the table erupted in laughter.

"The accordion! Do they even still make accordions?" Keith whooped.

"Well, they must if Bob has one," said Emily. Inside she was giddy with relief. She could live with an accordion player.

Now it was Bob's turn to ask a question. He felt it was time to shake things up, given the atmosphere the brothers had created to embarrass the players.

"Keith, have you always been faithful to your wife?"

"Whoa!" shouted Arthur. "Back at you, little brother."

"I'm not going to answer that," Keith stated grimly.

"Dare! Dare!" his sisters shouted.

"Then I dare you to sniff the armpits of everyone in this room," Bob said, thinking this was a pretty mild dare and should create more humor than distemper.

"No prob," Keith replied and lost the frown. He then good-naturedly went around the table, and as he reached each person, they raised an arm and let him sniff.

"Sorry I took a shower," Arthur commented, as Keith returned to his seat.

"Now it's my turn, and I have a similar question for Helen. Did you ever cheat on your husband?"

The four from next door, now working on third and fourth glasses of wine, were mostly amused at this question being asked again.

Helen went paler than she already was. "I'll take the dare," she whispered.

"No one knows you like your family," Keith hissed. "I dare you to eat leftover Brussel sprouts from tonight's dinner. Eat five. Right now! Out of the refrigerator."

Helen clutched her stomach and doubled over. "No, please, not that," she whispered.

The four guests looked on, mystified at her pain.

Seeing their expressions of confusion, Arthur explained. "When we were children, my father made Helen eat her vegetables at dinnertime, but they didn't always agree with her. He made her eat them anyway. They used to come back up, and he'd get mad. So she'd clamp her hands across her mouth, and the vomit would come out her nose. It was horrible to watch. She would be crying the whole time, with this green goo running down her face. Then he'd send her to her room for the rest of the night. Since she's been an adult, she won't eat vegetables at all."

"Not cooked vegetables," Angie corrected him. "She likes salad, which we never had as children."

"Well, Helen," said Keith, "If you won't answer my question, and you won't eat Brussel sprouts, then you'll have to take the penalty."

"Wait," said Angie. "I'll take her dare for her. There's a hurricane outside!"

"That's not in the rules," Arthur shouted.

"Well, it is now," Angie replied and stood up. She walked over to the kitchen area, opened the refrigerator, and showed everyone a bowl with the leftover Brussel sprouts. She removed the plastic covering, and picked out one with her fingers and popped it in her mouth.

"Yuck," said Keith. "I could never eat them cold."

But Angie kept going, and everyone silently watched as she ate four more. She then replaced the plastic wrap and put the bowl back in the refrigerator. "There," she said. "Done. Now I need another glass of wine."

"I think we should go now," Emily said. The mood in the room had changed. She motioned for her friends to get up from the table, and they started toward the door.

"Can I ask you a quick question before we go? Have the police resolved the problem with your father and the pajamas?"

"Get out!" Keith suddenly growled. "Our father is none of your business."

The four friends looked at each other in surprise and headed for the door.

"Yes, thank you. That was fun," Emily said as Bob opened the door. A strong gust of wind blew in, knocking over empty wine glasses and scattering bits of crackers and chips.

"Have a good trip home tomorrow," Angie called out as they left.

"You also," Elvis replied, the last to leave.

The foursome went out into the blustery darkness. They ran cautiously across the water-soaked grass and macadam between the two houses, wrestling their umbrellas against the wind.

"That was a weird evening," Elvis said, once they were safe inside their cottage."

"I'm so glad it's over," sighed Bob. "I felt like I was in a den of snakes."

"At least we survived," said Emily. "But we still don't know if their father was murdered, and if so, by whom. Guess we'll never know."

"That's not like us," Melinda said. "Maybe we'll learn something tomorrow."

"Right now, I'm too tired to care," Emily said. "The wine has made me sleepy."

In unison, she and Bob said, "Good night," and Emily dove into bed without a thought of the Skinnards.

CHAPTER FIFTEEN

THE RECKONING

Helen was dreaming.

She was a child again. She lay in bed in Chalet House, clutching her cloth doll, Raggedy Ann, for comfort. The wind was screaming outside, and pine boughs were banging against the windows. Keith stuck his head in the door.

"When will Mom and Dad be home?" she asked him.

"Soon. They're just playing cards next door."

"I'm afraid."

"Don't be."

Lightning flashed by the window and lit up the sky. The thunder followed immediately with a crash that shook the house. Helen thought she could hear the dishes rattling in the cupboards and the furniture jumping from their safe moorings on the floor. Angie screamed from her crib in their parents' room.

"I have to check on the baby," Keith said and left her alone.

Angie continued to cry despite Keith's best efforts to soothe her. Helen could hear him singing to her, a soft croon like the gurgle of a creek beneath the steady pounding of the rain on the roof. Helen was thankful for the night-light in the corner and the hall light at the top of the stairs, where her parents would appear any minute now. She was sure of it. She kept her eyes on the crack in the door and the light in the hallway.

The lightning came again, with the thunder on top of it. Helen remembered that if you counted "1 and 2 and 3" after the flash and before the thunder, that number would tell you how many miles away the storm was. She knew that no number meant the storm was on top of you. She wasn't afraid, she told herself. She wasn't afraid. Keith was here. He always took care of them.

But the lightning filled the room now, and the thunder was all around. Helen thought the house was going to explode. There was a crack and a boom, so loud, SO LOUD! SHE WAS SO SCARED! She heard Angie scream like she was dying, and then all the lights went out. Helen cried out, "Help me! Ah, ah, ah...!" She was going to die!

Emily couldn't sleep. The events at Chalet House kept playing over and over in her head. Something had happened to Mr. Skinnard, maybe murder. Emily needed to know. And if it was murder, the killer needed to be brought to justice.

Bob snored softly beside her. He had dropped off to sleep quickly once they'd gotten to bed. She wondered if Melinda and Elvis were also asleep.

After twenty minutes of worried tossing and turning, she decided to get up. Tweaked by intuition, she put on a sweatshirt and jeans. Then she softly padded out of the bedroom and down the stairs. Cautiously putting one foot in front of the other to avoid any noise, she thought she finally understood what the ghost had been trying to say.

She found Melinda in the living room seated on the floor in a crossed-leg yoga pose. She also had on jeans and a sweatshirt. Her eyes were closed.

"You're up too," Emily whispered.

Melinda opened her eyes. "Yes. I'm worried about what's happening next door. I think we should go back over there."

"In this storm?"

"Take a listen. The storm's over."

Emily cocked her head, and the silence surprised her.

"What would be our excuse for disturbing them at this hour?"

"Let's say you lost your inhaler for your asthma and it might have fallen out of your purse when you were there earlier. That seems urgent enough."

"But I don't have an inhaler."

"They don't know that."

"Okay. Should we wake the guys?"

"No time."

"Melinda, I think I know what the ghost meant when he appeared to me. He was saying, 'Help Helen.'"

"Then we'd better hurry."

They quietly put on shoes and let themselves out into the night. The world was dead quiet. Trees stood still, the insects were silent, and the moon was a sliver in a starless sky. As they crossed the driveway between the two houses, they heard a scream.

Helen woke from her dream a little before midnight. She was shivering and felt almost as frightened now as she had as a child. She thought back to Hurricane Carol in 1954, on this same date, August 31.

Although the storm outside had abated, it swirled still in Helen's imagination. Her head throbbed from the roar of the wind. She felt the sting of the rain on her face. She staggered from her room as the howling in her head echoed the hurt in her heart. In her mind, the rain poured down like the tears she could not shed for the life she could not mourn, because she would never know what might have been. She could have howled with anger—anger that had been building in her for years—at the man who had died.

Helen entered her father's room on tiptoe and stood still, looking at the empty bed, remembering.

She had seen her father easily enough, late Monday night, in the glow of the night-light from the hallway. He had been naked under a light sheet. In her hands were yellow pajama pants. She had gently placed one leg of the pajama pants underneath her father's neck and pulled it out the other side. So deep was his sleep, he never stirred. Then she began to twist that pajama leg around the other leg, thinking to tie a knot with the two legs and strangle him in his sleep. She was shaking and near to crying. She didn't want to do this. Part of her loved this man who had read poems to her when she was a child.

But another part remembered that Christmas morning when she and Angie had waited with bated breath to see the look of joy on their mother's face when she opened their present. Their gift, wrapped in simple white tissue paper, had been specially chosen: delicately embroidered yellow pajamas.

And their mother *had* smiled at first when she saw the pretty jewel neckline decorated with eyelet and roses. But they'd watched her smile fade as she saw that it was a top and not a gown. Then she picked up the pants and started to cry. "Oh, girls," she said, tears streaming down both her cheeks. "Your father won't *let* me wear pajamas."

Helen had been confused. At fifteen, she didn't know much about sex, but as she watched her mother's tears, she knew that shame accompanied it, and obligation, and control. It was a Christmas she never forgot.

Now, in the early hours of Saturday morning, in the aftermath of the storm, she remembered how she had taken the pajama legs and tied them together under her father's chin. As she had pulled to tighten the knot, the air in the bedroom had turned cold. Even now, she could feel its icy fingers first on her neck then caressing her exposed wrists and ankles, even creeping up in between her legs.

That night was when she had seen it—a ghostly shadow that shimmered in a soft silvery light on the opposite side of the bed. As she watched, hardly believing what was happening, the form of a man had emerged. The face was indistinct, but she clearly saw an arm reach out to her and place its hand on hers. Its touch felt like expensive silk, soft and liquid. Her body had reacted without thought; she had let go of the pajamas and jumped back. She was surprised to find that she was not terrified, only stunned. No words had come to her; she made no sound. And, within seconds, the ghost had begun to dissipate.

In her reverie, Helen became aware of noises from downstairs, but she was too consumed with her memory to react.

She had gazed down at her father—she could still remember him lying there—and how he had opened his eyes. He had not moved a muscle but stared right up at her, fixing her with his pale blue eyes, rheumy and wide. She had thought, *He knows what I want to do!*

He had struggled to take in air, managed a breath, and rested. Then he had smiled, his grin thin and evil—a conspirator's smile.

Helen had gone cold inside and remembered *her* infidelities that had ruined her marriage, something she had spent half a lifetime trying to forget. She may not have been as profligate or as tyrannical as her father, but she had caused pain to her spouse and her children, nonetheless.

She had become overwhelmed with waves of guilt. Then her mind, which felt like an angry train speeding and pounding through her head, had changed tracks again and told her that his sins far outnumbered hers. He was the man responsible for the frightened woman she had become. She forgot the specter she had seen, picked up the pajamas again, and began to pull the knot tighter.

Behind her, the door had burst open. Hands had reached around her and covered her own, stopping her from completing her task.

"Helen, no!" Angie had shouted, her arms encircling Helen's waist.

But it was too late; their father was dead.

Helen looked at the bed. Empty now. She realized she was reliving her father's death. And she screamed, seized with the horror of what had happened.

What did I do? Did I kill my father? Will I be punished for it? She prayed that death take her, painless and instantaneous.

She heard noises downstairs.

Suddenly, the memory of what had happened next, after Angie had thrown her arms around her, had come back to her. "Help me," she cried out.

Her brothers had come into the room as Mr. Skinnard had gasped one last time and, then, no more.

Struck silent, the siblings had gazed at Mr. Skinnard's lifeless body. Helen saw the white sheet covering him start to transform into long irregular shapes. As she watched, hardly believing what she was witnessing, the irregular shapes became jagged oblongs and, then, the oblongs became feathers. As the feathers increased in number, they formed two broad white wings. Two enormous angel wings that enfolded her father. It took her a moment to understand that an angel was embracing her father right before her eyes.

How dare God! had been Helen's first thought. *He doesn't deserve to be saved.*

Helen's mind had rebelled at the idea of forgiveness without penance. But as she gazed at her father swathed in white feathery wings, she had found comfort in the thought that, in death, there was redemption. And if there were redemption for her father, perhaps there would be redemption for her.

Then as suddenly as they had appeared, the angel wings vanished, and the frail shell of their father had lain in quiet repose.

"What the hell just happened here?" Arthur had finally said.

"I know what I saw, but I don't trust my eyes," Keith had replied. "We're all tired and upset. Perhaps it's the flickering light from the streetlamps outside." He had turned to Helen. "Did you kill him?"

"I had to," Helen had said.

"How could you?" hissed Arthur. "He was our father."

"He was a monster to our mother," Angie had said. "I imagine we've all wanted to kill him at some point. I need to call 911 now."

Angie had removed the pajama bottom from around her father's neck and thrown it on a chair. But she couldn't think of what to do to disguise the blotches around her father's neck. "We tell the police he died of natural causes," Angie had said to her brothers. "Helen is not going to jail."

Helen, sobbing, pressed her hands to her head to dislodge her memories.

Emily and Melinda burst into the bedroom now, having broken away from Keith as he'd tried to stop them from going upstairs. Keith and Arthur followed them in.

"I didn't mean to kill him," Helen cried to them when they entered the room.

Emily and Melinda stood motionless as Helen quietly told them what she had done the night her father died.

"It doesn't matter," Arthur said as they stood staring at the empty bed. "The autopsy result came back this afternoon. What with the hurricane and all, I forgot to tell you. He died of heart failure, not strangulation. We're free to leave."

"No!" wailed Helen. "After he drove me to it. After he taunted me. I didn't even kill him?"

Helen looked around the room and saw, in the pitying eyes of the others, that she was in a drama of her own making, with herself as the victim again. She couldn't bear the humiliation. She fled the room in tears.

Returning to their cottage, Emily said to Melinda, "Angie's dream last Saturday wasn't quite right, was it? Someone did die, but no one was murdered."

"Helen wanted to kill her father. Luckily, Angie was able to stop her," Melinda replied. "Maybe that's what the dream was all about."

"Maybe. And when you saw the siblings tonight, were they adults or children?"

"Adults all, very sad adults."

Back in Chalet House, the spirit of the house had noted the death of Mr. Skinnard and Helen's confrontation with her shared guilt and innocence. As Frank saw it, his job was now done.

SATURDAY

CHAPTER SIXTEEN
THE QUESTION

Angie was cleaning up the kitchen when she noticed that the air in the house felt lighter. Perhaps the storm had cleansed the atmosphere not only of heavy moisture but also heavy thoughts. She saw Keith coming down the stairs with his suitcase and waited for him at the bottom. When he got there, she put her arms around him and said, "I love you."

Startled, Keith smiled and returned her hug. "Love you too," he replied.

When Arthur came in from outside, she stopped him and hugged him, saying the same words, "I love you." He shook her off but smiled like Keith. "You know I love you, sis."

Arthur looked up and saw his baseball cap perched on the coat rack. He picked up the cap and turned it over in his hands, musing out loud, "Where have you been, and how did you get back here?"

Seeing this, Keith turned around to the sideboard and saw his keys sitting in the bowl where'd he left them six days ago.

"My keys are here too," he said. "Very strange."

Helen came downstairs in time to see Angie and Arthur smiling at each other. She put down her suitcase and put her arms around them both. "Love you guys," she said.

Keith, seeing the three standing there, walked over to embrace his siblings. "We'll be alright," he said.

"Mom would be so happy to see us together like this," Helen commented as the four resumed their tasks of readying the house for departure.

"Y'all come to my house for Thanksgiving," Arthur said. "We've plenty of room."

"And my house for Christmas," Angie offered.

"What about Ted's family?" Helen asked.

"They'll have to get used to seeing you," Angie replied.

Next door, the four friends were also preparing to leave. The TV droned in the background as they emptied the refrigerator and packed the unused food.

"Listen up," Elvis suddenly announced. "On the news."

The other three followed his command and looked at the TV where a news anchor was reporting events following the storm. Behind him was a photograph of a younger-looking Mervin Crippens.

"Also in the news this morning," the anchor said, "the body of eighty-five-year-old Mervin Crippens was found in his hotel room dead of what appears to be a self-inflicted gunshot wound. Mr. Crippens was a native of Dover who had a long career in industrial security. He seems to have died at the height of the storm last night. The police say it appears to be suicide."

"Wow!" Bob blurted out. "How strange is that? And we were just talking about him to the Smiths the other night."

Emily looked at Melinda as the same thought occurred to each. *Were they responsible for alerting Dan Smith to Crippins's presence in Rehoboth?* Neither said a word.

As if reading their thoughts, Bob said, "Luckily, we can alibi the Skinnards for last night."

"And what about Dan Smith?" asked Elvis. "Do you think he had a hand in it?"

"Not our problem," said Emily. Melinda smiled in agreement.

All went back to packing up the kitchen.

After Bob and Elvis had stowed their suitcases in their respective cars, Elvis said, "I have a request to make. One more thing I'd like to do before we leave Rehoboth."

"Okay by me," Bob answered. "But we're supposed to be out of here by 11 a.m. per the rental agreement."

"I think the storm has altered all that," Emily responded. "It'll be slow going getting out of Rehoboth, although according to the news, there was surprisingly little damage. Some sand has been lost on the beach, and a few sheds were blown down, but on the whole, Rehoboth weathered the storm quite well."

"I don't think Edgar even made it to a Category 1 storm," Elvis added.

"Thank goodness," Melinda said.

"What is it you want to do?" she asked.

"I want to go down to the beach," he said. "I want to take one last look at the ocean before we go."

"No problem for me," Bob said. "I'd like to do that too. I'm curious to see if there's any damage from the storm."

The four finished their last cups of coffee, started the dishwasher, and locked up the house. Then they glanced over at Chalet House. All was quiet there.

"I wish I could say good-bye," Emily said. "But I think it's better not to disturb them."

"They need any sleep they can get," Melinda said. "Poor kids."

The four got into their cars and headed down Oak Avenue toward the beach. They had to negotiate a fallen tree limb, but they saw no real damage to the cottages along the way.

At the bottom of the road, a few cars were parked around the entrance to the beach. Others were as curious as they were to see how the beach had fared after the storm. The dunes were wet and the sand firm, so it was easy to climb the path in between the dune grass, over and down to the shoreline.

The usual detritus had washed up after a storm: driftwood, shells, and abandoned horseshoe crab casings. There were unsightly plastic bags and six-pack holders, plastic bottles and beer cans, even a few disposable baby diapers.

The ocean itself was still angry, with white foam waves of ten and twelve feet towering over the shore below, and then folding in upon themselves to come crashing down on the sand. The sun shone on dark water where blue-green currents moved swiftly along the coast in a riptide that swimmers would be foolish to challenge.

"I've seen enough," said Emily. "Let's go back to the car."

She turned around, but Bob caught her arm and whispered, "Wait."

And, then, she saw Elvis, down on one knee, in front of Melinda.

"This wasn't quite the scene I was hoping for," he said. "I pictured a calm day, with the sun shining and the water gently lapping on the beach, but this will have to do."

"Do for what?" Melinda asked, but by her smile, Emily could tell that she knew what was coming.

Elvis pulled a small box from his pocket and opened it. Bob and Emily's curiosity overcame their good manners. They leaned forward and saw the ruby ring Melinda had admired in the Lewes antique store. They would have sworn from Melinda's gasp of recognition that she was as equally surprised as Emily was. Bob had known about it ever since Elvis had bought the ring after their fishing trip on Thursday.

"Elvis, this is too much," Melinda gasped.

He didn't answer but merely said, "Melinda, my most beautiful lady, make me the happiest man in the world and be my wife."

"Yes, of course," she said softly.

He slipped the ring on her finger, and the ruby's red fire appeared to leap out and glow with all the passion and promise of the two hearts it joined together.

"And they *will* live happily ever after," Emily whispered to Bob as Melinda and Elvis kissed.

THE END

MOM

A Poem by Helen Skinnard

"Some days I can't remember what she looked like,"
My sister said and ran her finger 'round
The rim of her martini. She turned to me.
"And you?" she asked with moisture in her eye.
"I see her every morning in the mirror,
The silver hair, the heavy jaw, the nose.
Unlike you, I can't seem to escape her."

Our mother was a kind and careful creature,
Warm hug, quick kiss, a whispered word of love.
A shadow-dweller soothing all things over,
Skinned knees, teasing brothers, angry fathers.
And when she could not soothe, she would flee.

Upstairs, behind closed doors, under covers,
We heard her sobs and shrunk into ourselves.
Five siblings looking scared one to each other,
Abandoned ducklings temporarily lost at sea.
Perhaps forgetfulness is healing for my sister.
On me, the familiar face has found a kinder life
And a radar for bullies that rarely lets me down.

Follow the clues with Emily Menotti as she unravels still more mysteries:

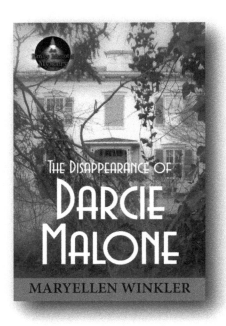

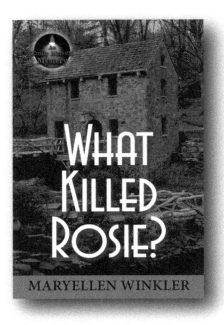

On a warm September night in 1969, a young couple embarks on a romantic picnic on the grounds of a reputedly haunted house. By morning, the young girl has disappeared, and her boyfriend is found mentally confused and unable to speak. The girl is never found, and the mystery is never resolved.

Thirty years later, a woman stands in the dark and hears an old man singing, "Darcie Malone, Darcie Malone, Darcie, why don't you come home?" She turns to see who is singing, but no one is there.

Darcie Malone is the young woman who went missing in 1969. Emily Menotti, intrigued by the old man's plaintive song, begins to investigate what happened on that long-ago night. Along the way, she'll meet Darcie's elderly mother and strange brother, an ambitious reporter, local ghost hunters, and the original detective assigned to the case in 1969.

Who did Emily see in the laundromat doorway that warm May evening? It looked like her old friend Rosie. Problem is, Rosie died of a heart attack five years ago.

Rosie's old boyfriend is reporting strange occurrences at his condo. Is it Rosie's ghost demanding revenge? Or is someone trying to perpetrate a hoax?

Join Emily as she searches among Rosie's acquaintances to find out what really killed Rosie.

Emily's previous adventures are available at
The Hockessin Book Shelf and Amazon.com.

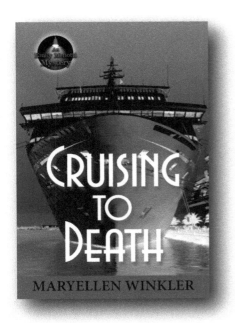

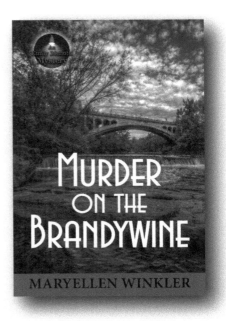

Intrepid amateur sleuth, Emily Menotti, is on her first Caribbean cruise along with the Wayward Sisters book club. As they head out of New York City, however, a friend goes missing.

With the help of her clairsentient pal, Melinda, Emily starts investigating. Yet even a séance, guided by Melinda, reveals more old secrets than new clues.

Set amid tropical backdrops, this mystery has motives aplenty, including an ex-husband, a former high school boyfriend, and the on-going resentment of two unmarried friends.

Join Emily as she solves the mystery on a chilling cruise with some uninvited passengers: jealousy, revenge, and death.

A beautiful young woman, Alicia Kingston, is on the verge of having her dreams come true. Engaged to be married, she is drawn into a revolutionary group that plans to strike a blow against the evils of the 1990s banking industry. But one Sunday morning, she is found murdered in Brandywine Creek State Park.

Mirety Bank, a major player in the predatory lending practices, is Alicia's employer. Also working there is Emily Menotti, the woman who discovers Alicia's body. Is the mysterious tattoo of an owl on Alicia's back tied to her death? As Emily investigates, Alicia's fiancée, her brother, and higher-ups in the bank all become suspects.

Emily's search revives all her favorite memories of living in Wilmington and the Brandywine Valley. Follow in her footsteps as she tracks down the killer and ends up fighting for both her job and her life.

CPSIA information can be obtained
at www.ICGtesting.com
Printed in the USA
BVHW092113270922
648007BV00011B/33

9 781935 751120